Walking Mary

ALSO BY JAMES VANOOSTING

The Last Payback

James VanOosting

Walking Mary

HarperCollinsPublishers

Walking Mary
Copyright © 2005 by James VanOosting

www.harperchildrens.com

Library of Congress Cataloging-in-Publication Data

VanOosting, James.
   Walking Mary / James VanOosting.—1st ed.
     p.   cm.

   Summary: To escape problems with both of her parents throughout her childhood in the 1940s and 1950s, Pearl Harbor Keenan reaches out to Walking Mary, a strange old woman who meets every single passenger train that pulls into the Framburg depot.

   ISBN 0-06-028471-4 — ISBN 0-06-028472-2 (lib. bdg.)

   [1. Eccentrics and eccentricities—Fiction. 2. Family problems—Fiction. 3. Railroads—Trains—Fiction. 4. Old age—Fiction. 5. Toleration—Fiction. 6. African Americans—Fiction.] I. Title.

PZ7.V3425Wal 2005
[Fic]—dc22

2004021500
CIP
AC

Typography by Karin Paprocki
1 2 3 4 5 6 7 8 9 10

First Edition

To my sister Kathi,
without whom I doubt the safe passage
from child to adult

And

To my wife, the Dawn
of my late-blooming maturity

Acknowledgments

WALKING MARY IS A NOVEL I've taken thirty years to write. I began writing it before any other book I published, and I couldn't get it right. Then I tried it again between published books—that's nine separate versions, all having nothing in common beyond a simple narrative core. The character of Walking Mary actually dates to my early childhood. And the only other thing I knew for sure throughout every version was that it would take a sister and a brother to understand her. I just didn't realize that that understanding would require thirty years of effort, disparate narratives, considerable pain, occasional joy, and the support of so many friends. I want to say several thank-yous.

THANKS TO INSIGHTFUL READERS: Peter VanOosting, Thomas VanOosting, Lynn Miller, Alexandria Williams, Peg Oosting, Laura Weant, and Alanna Carter.

Thanks to Sharon Taylor, who trusted this story and its author during the bleakest years.

Thanks to literary agent George Nicholson, who's always believed in my writerly voice.

Thanks to editors Margaret Ferguson and Ginee Seo, who went as far as they could, and to the indescribable Ruth Katcher, who finished the race with me. Ultimately, she saw the story as I could not. My thanks also to the excellent copyediting of Janet Frick and Ellen Leach.

And, finally, my loving gratitude to the two women to whom I dedicate this book, Kathi Best and Dawn Williams.

Walking Mary

One

P EARL KEENAN WAS BORN on December 7, 1941, and her mother named her "Pearl Harbor" by pure accident. Mrs. Keenan was lying in a hospital bed listening to the crackling voice of President Roosevelt coming over WQFR radio and, to her ears, he was proclaiming, "This is a day that shall live in *symphony*." Well, "a day that shall live in symphony" was just about the fanciest expression Pearl's mother had ever heard, and she fell asleep expecting to hear something called "The Pearl Harbor Symphony," which never happened because President Roosevelt never used the word *symphony*. It was *infamy*.

When Mrs. Keenan found out her mistake—how she'd named her daughter after an act of war—she felt absolutely horrible. From that day on, everybody called the girl just plain Pearl. "A pearl of great price, mind you," her mother sometimes reminded her, but the two of them buried that

"Harbor" between them.

Less than two years later, bang in the middle of World War II, Pearl's little brother came along. The name on the boy's birth certificate was Franklin, same as their father, but there was disagreement from the get-go whether "Franklin" or "Frankie" sounded better. Different family members went back and forth, depending.

So there was the basic group—mother, father, older sister, and little brother, with an occasional dog, a rabbit, a few chicks on one regrettable Easter morning, and a box turtle named Molly who could turn around in a circle, counterclockwise, if you banged on her shell hard enough with a stick.

On Memorial Day weekend 1948, Pearl was nearly six and a half years old, Frankie just five. Like just about everybody else in Framburg, the Keenan family was enjoying a picnic in Veterans' Park. This location did not include the Negroes, who displayed their holiday patriotism in their own park on the east side of the Pecatonica River.

While their mother unpacked the food, Mr. Keenan sent Pearl and Frankie down to the pond to feed the ducks. The children had never gone to the pond all on their own before, so they felt grown-up and grateful for the opportunity.

As they were walking toward the duck pond, which was out of sight of their parents, Pearl took hold of Frankie's hand and said, helpfully, "A duck will bite your finger clean off if you don't watch out."

This was news to Frankie, who asked, "Really?" and right there and then decided it was all right for Pearl to keep such a tight hold on his hand. He possessed ten fingers and didn't intend to let a duck bite any of them clean off.

"Oh sure, everybody knows that. Becky Shasker had a cousin get her finger bit clean off by a duck."

Franklin was just five years old, but he happened to have a skeptical mind and was not easily fooled. "Were you there?" he asked.

"No, but Becky told me about it. Chomp. The duck bit her cousin's finger off, just like that. Don't you believe me?"

"Did you at least *see* the finger?"

"There was nothing to see, Frankie. The duck ate it."

Frankie had not considered this obvious possibility, and he suddenly realized how much of the world he had never been exposed to. He wondered what else he didn't know that might possibly cause him pain or loss of body parts. He wished he could be six years old and know as much as Pearl. Sometimes he believed if he could just get himself a pair of eyeglasses, like the ones Pearl wore, he would become instantly smarter, but he had failed to fail the eye exam at Dr. Smith's office and wasn't allowed to wear any eyeglasses.

Pearl had a kind heart, so she added, "Our ducks at Veterans' Park don't bite little boys' fingers off. It's against the law in Framburg."

The pond was pretty as a postcard. Standing at the edge of the water, the children didn't see any ducks. Pearl said, "They must be down by the bridge."

The pond at Veterans' Park pushes against the land to form a letter *V*. At the notch of the *V* stands a monster oak tree. Pearl sidled up next to its broad trunk, Frankie squeezed in next to her, and they both peered around the curve of the thick bark. Ten yards ahead of them and not far from the bridge were all of the town's ducks together. There must have been close to a hundred of them. Some of the ducks were on the water; others were on the shore. All of the ducks were looking up toward the same spot.

"What the heck?" Pearl whispered, which was a very strong word for her to use on account of being a Baptist. She eased herself around the oak tree to get a better view. Frankie inched along behind. Just as soon as Frankie spotted Walking Mary, he screamed, "Run for your life!" Even a five-year-old knew that much.

Little Frankie took his own good advice. He ran for his life for about twenty steps, until he noticed that there weren't any other feet running behind him, so he had to stop.

From where he was standing, Frankie could see that Pearl was staring straight at Walking Mary, the old lady who met all the trains. Any child knew never to stare at Walking Mary unless you wanted to get turned into a garter snake or, more likely, an iguana. Walking Mary was standing about ten feet back from the water and not more than twenty feet from the oak tree. Her thin-as-wire arms were spread wide, lifted to a height parallel to the ground, and she was flapping them in slow repetition, down to her sides and back up again. When she moved, her old mink coat rustled rhythmically like the wings of a bat in flight, and its lining gleamed.

Frankie ran back toward his sister and grabbed her around the waist. This was the bravest thing he had ever done. "Let's beat it!" he yelled.

At the sound of Frankie's voice, Walking Mary locked her arms at their highest reach. Her body appeared to be carved out of stone, but her head was quick, jerking in the direction of the oak tree. She looked right past Frankie and fixed her eyes on Pearl. Then she swooped her arms down and started walking straight toward the children. Frankie did not mean to abandon his sister, letting go and stepping away, but he also did not mean to get turned into an iguana or a snake.

Frankie yelled, "She's a witch!" as a reminder to his sister, in case she had lost her mind and forgotten who Walking Mary really was.

Frankie could not have been more scared by the Devil himself when he stopped and turned around to watch Walking Mary transform his sister into an iguana.

But Walking Mary did *not* turn Pearl into an iguana. As Walking Mary approached, Pearl took cautious steps backward. Suddenly, she slipped on the muddy bank of the pond and fell into the water up to her waist. Walking Mary hurried forward to the water's edge and stretched out her crooked hands to Pearl. Pearl took one more step back and must have hit a deep spot, because she disappeared completely, head and all, under the water. Frankie gasped. Then Walking Mary stepped right into the water after Pearl, mink coat and everything.

The old lady pulled Pearl up from the water, looking just like John the Baptizer standing in the River Jordan in that painting on the wall of the Sunday School room. Frankie saw Walking Mary touch both of Pearl's ears with her old brown fingers, and Pearl just stood there, not even trying to pull away. Then he saw Walking Mary touch both of Pearl's eyes and place her brown fingers right over Pearl's mouth, tracing the outline of his sister's shivering lips. And then he saw Walking Mary smooth back Pearl's wet hair, just like a mother would do, if anybody could picture Walking Mary as a mother, which Frankie certainly could not.

That was all Frankie saw before he peed his pants, which sent him into a panic because this wasn't supposed to happen anymore. He ran back to the family's picnic spot without his sister, who had been touched by Walking Mary, and could never be untouched so long as she lived. Frankie calculated this wouldn't be for very long now, and he felt sad.

WHEN PEARL ARRIVED back at the family picnic spot, she was dripping wet. Frankie had already told the story about Walking Mary, but nobody had believed him.

"What happened, honey?" their father said to Pearl.

"Where are your glasses?" their mother asked.

Pearl reached up and felt for her glasses, which weren't there.

"I must have lost them when I fell into the pond," she said.

"That's okay," their father said. He stepped closer to Pearl and put his arm around his pretty little daughter.

But Frankie wasn't paying attention to their daddy just then. Instead, he was staring openmouthed at Walking Mary, who had appeared very close by, just the other side of a chestnut tree. She stood watching the whole family directly and without blinking.

"What are you staring at?" their daddy snapped at the boy.

"Nothing," Frankie answered.

"Well, I should hope not," their daddy said, letting loose of Pearl.

Frankie had never seen Walking Mary smile before. Her teeth were yellowish.

Two

WALKING MARY WAS AN old lady—nobody knew exactly how old—who couldn't have stood more than five feet tall, with wrinkled skin the color of shaved chocolate before you add the warm milk to make cocoa. Her hands were too large for so slight a body, appearing more chiseled than wrinkled. Tissue-paper skin wrapped around her swollen knuckles and veins. Walking Mary's eyes were a deep gray with teeny blue flecks flashing out suddenly and unexpectedly like hot sparks. Some people compared them to a cat's eyes, others to a bird's, especially to the eyes of a hawk. One particular story had it that Walking Mary was blind in one of her eyes, although there was disagreement about which one, and not everybody believed this anyway. Another tale held that she could roll those eyes of hers—at least the one good one—straight up into their sockets, revealing the watery yellow backsides of her eyeballs. None of these details was easy to confirm, because all Framburgers—children and adults alike—subscribed to one universal rule of public safety: *Never look Walking Mary straight in the eye.* She could cast spells. Everybody agreed on that.

After her ducking at Veterans' Park, Pearl didn't need glasses anymore to see clearly. This fact came as a shock to everybody who knew about it, which wasn't very many on account of how Mrs. Keenan warned the family not to say a word about it. Mother took Pearl to Dr. Smith, the eye doctor, who examined the girl's eyes, and certified it was a miracle how she didn't need glasses anymore, and he couldn't possibly sell Mrs. Keenan another pair under false pretenses. Although Pearl's mother was a good Baptist and certainly believed in miracles, it violated theology to witness a healing having occurred in her own respectable family. So she took Pearl to Framburg's other eye doctor, Dr. Wolfe. Dr. Wolfe confirmed that Pearl did not need glasses, and Mrs. Keenan became convinced her daughter had not required eyeglasses in the first place. This was a very sensible explanation for what couldn't be explained, so she told Pearl that the word *miracle* should not be uttered aloud because it was inappropriate to the circumstances.

Frankie had his own theory, but at age five he did not

possess the vocabulary to explain or defend it to anyone except Pearl. Their two bedrooms were on the second story of the house, where there weren't any other rooms except the bath, and their two bedrooms were connected by one big closet with a high window. One night, Pearl and Frankie met inside this closet, which they often did secretly.

"You didn't ever need eyeglasses in the first place," Frankie accused his sister.

"Did so," Pearl answered back. "And don't talk so loud, Franklin."

"But Mother said . . . "

"Mother doesn't know. I should know. They're my eyes, aren't they?"

"Yes," Frankie admitted.

"I didn't used to see except with glasses, and now I can see without any glasses. I don't ever lie. And you know that to be the truth."

Frankie did know this. His sister never lied.

The boy sat quietly, contemplating. Mother must have got confused, he concluded, which was a hard fact to accept. So then he went ahead and confessed his theory, whispering.

"*She* did it, didn't she, Pearl?"

"Who?" Pearl whispered back.

"Her. Walking Mary."

"How could she have done it?" Pearl asked.

"Magic," Frankie said.

"Well, I don't believe in magic, and neither should you."

"A magic *spell*," Frankie insisted, sounding magical and mysterious with his own voice. "That's what she did when she pulled you up out of the water. She cast a magic spell over your whole body, and that includes your eyes."

Pearl did not answer, and Frankie took this to mean she accepted his theory.

"How do your ears feel?" Frankie wanted to know. "Maybe you have superhearing, too." He recalled how Walking Mary had touched his sister's ears and her lips, as well as her eyes.

Pearl reached out and punched Frankie in the shoulder, causing him to topple over, which did not seem entirely necessary to him. Frankie could not say whether this was the first time the idea of a magic spell had occurred to Pearl, and she did not volunteer her own explanation for what had happened to her in the duck pond. But this idea of a spell cast by Walking Mary over his sister was not one that departed easily from Frankie's mind.

NINE MONTHS LATER, TOWARD the end of February, when Frankie was still five years old, he received further proof that his sister was now living under the spell of Walking Mary. The boy was not proud of how he came by this information because it included two big sins—spying and nakedness.

One Friday, Pearl's friend Francine came over to spend the night at the Keenans' house. Before bedtime, the two girls took a bath together. Earlier in the afternoon, Pearl had told Frankie to get lost, and, naturally, Frankie had not taken his sister's uppity attitude sitting down. So he did not feel guilty when he climbed up onto the top of his dresser and peeked down through the hole in his bedroom wall where their father had never yet repaired the molding, and looked into the bathroom where his sister and her friend were settling into a deep tub.

He could hear what they were saying very clearly, and he could see everything that was going on.

"Let's play baptism," Pearl suggested.

"How do you do that?" Francine asked.

Pearl raised her eyebrows. "Shhhhh, don't talk so loud. I'll show you."

Pearl was an expert in all things regarding baptism, same as the rest of the family, because this was the religious specialty of their Framburg Baptist Fellowship. Francine, by contrast, was a Catholic, which meant she didn't know beans about religion, especially an item as complicated as baptism, which Frankie had on good authority from their father, who did not favor Catholics under any circumstances except, naturally, as customers in his bank.

Frankie was kneeling on top of his dresser, and he inched one way and another to settle in for as long as the girls' mock baptismal service might last. Pearl and Francine were sitting in the tub facing each other.

(No one should misjudge Frankie for what he was doing or thinking, although spying on one's sister is never an altogether proper thing to do. If he had been twelve years old instead of just five, or if this episode were taking place today instead of back then, one might imagine what thoughts would have been going through his mind. But such imaginings were *not* the case. What interested Franklin Keenan was intelligence gathering, pure and simple, and that's the bare truth.)

"If you take your baptism by sprinkling," Pearl instructed Francine, "it works like this."

Frankie watched his sister dip the fingers of her right hand into the water and lift them to eye level, then heard her speak these holy words. "In the name of the Father, and of the Son, and of the Holy Ghost." With each phrase, Pearl flicked a few drops of water into Francine's face. At the climax, she spritzed her good and pronounced, "I baptize you Miss Hermanson," who was the name of their gym teacher. It was quite comical for Pearl to baptize Francine as Miss Hermanson, but Frankie knew better than to laugh and give himself away.

"Okay, I get it now," Francine said. She wiped off her face, then splashed her own hand into the holy water to gather a fistful. "Like this?"

"Be careful," Pearl warned, scootching back a few inches and setting a rolling wave into motion.

Francine sat up tall and rigid, like a minister might. "In the name of the Father, and of the Son, and of the Holy Ghost," she said in a singsong, "I baptize you Mrs. Wesson." Mrs. Wesson was their oily second-grade teacher, on whom Frankie had a silent crush. Nobody else at Lincoln Elementary even liked her, so he knew enough to keep his affection under wraps. At the sound of this new name, Francine let fly with what water remained in her tight fist.

Pearl giggled, wiping the holy drops off her face. "Of course, sprinkling's just for babies," she said, widening her smile, which Frankie recognized as a forecast of stormy weather to come. She leaned over the side of the tub and picked up a blue plastic cup used for rinsing shampoo. "Allow me to demonstrate." Pearl submerged the cup and filled it full. "Lean forward."

"Like this?" Francine inclined her head toward Pearl.

"In the name of the Father . . . " Pearl poured a little rivulet onto Francine's head, letting it run through her thin blond hair and onto her forehead. "And of the Son . . ." She poured a little more water, widening the stream so that Francine's bangs got wetted down and flattened. "And of the Holy Ghost . . ." Now the water began flowing like a river. "I baptize you Louise Fishback."

Frankie watched Pearl pour the rest of the water over Francine's head. He knew all about Louise Fishback. Who didn't? Louise Fishback was an overweight fourth grader who could press the contents of a peanut butter and jelly sandwich through her teeth. Pearl and Francine considered this trick grotesque. Frankie, on the other hand, admired Louise Fishback's talent and dreamed of replicating the performance himself someday. He had already started practicing.

"Not Louise," Francine protested, swallowing a mouthful of bath water. "That's unfair."

"Baptism is for sinners," Pearl explained. "So I figure Louise stands at the front of the line."

Francine grabbed the cup out of Pearl's hand and dipped it back into the tub. Being less practiced in the art of baptizing, Francine forgot the formula for pronouncing what you're supposed to say. "Here goes nothing," she improvised. "I baptize you Punch Connelly."

Frankie watched in delight as Francine emptied the entire cup on his sister's head. Water cascaded down all sides, plastering her long brown hair to her shoulders and back while drenching her face.

Punch Connelly could push jelly beans up his nose and keep them in there long enough to warm into streams of pink and green snot. His was the only name that could possibly have topped Louise Fishback, and Frankie appreciated the beauty of Francine's choice.

Pearl snatched the plastic cup away from her friend and plunked it over the side of the tub onto the floor. "As John the Baptist used to say," she announced, "anybody care to go for a dip?"

"What's that supposed to mean?" Francine asked.

"Don't you know about baptism by immersion?"

"You mean dunking?" Francine said. "I've seen it in a movie. I get to go first this time."

Frankie could tell Pearl was confused by her friend's enthusiasm. Pearl didn't like to get beaten at her own game, but what was she supposed to do, with Francine being her guest and all?

Francine pushed herself up onto her knees and placed both her hands on top of Pearl's head. All of a sudden, it was clear how much Francine had mastered the art of baptism, and Frankie marveled that a Catholic should grasp hold of this fundamental Baptist mystery.

"In the name of the Father, and of the Son, and of the Holy Ghost . . . " Francine paused, letting the Holy Ghost do its work, and then finished the job herself. "I baptize you Walking Mary."

As she pronounced the name to end all names, Francine hooted a loud laugh and pushed Pearl's head back clear under the water.

Frankie inched forward, pressing his face to the hole in the wall.

Pearl came up for air, giggling. "Whooo! What name did you call me? My ears were already underwater."

Francine repeated, "Walking Mary," and launched a surprise attack, dunking Pearl for a second time.

When she came back up, Pearl demanded, "Why did you call me *that*?"

"Because she's a witch, that's why." By now, Francine was laughing wildly.

"You're not allowed to baptize witches," Pearl complained. "It's against sacred scripture. And, anyhow, don't be calling her a witch. What do you know about Walking Mary?"

"Take it easy," Francine said soothingly, made nervous by Pearl's voice, which Frankie recognized as full of anger, hurt, and agitation.

"I take it back," said Francine. "I'll dunk you again with a different name if that'll make you feel better."

"No," Pearl complained, all the fun drained out of her voice now. "You can't take back a baptism. Once you've done a baptism, it's done for good. It sticks for all eternity."

That's when Frankie heard a loud knock on the bathroom door. He had not heard anyone come up the stairs. At the explosive sound, his hands slipped down the wall, and he almost lost his balance.

"Are you girls getting washed in there?" Mr. Keenan asked.

At the sound of her father's voice, Pearl looked up toward the tiny hole in the wall. Suddenly, Frankie was doused with a flood of guilt. What had he been doing, for gosh sake? He looked down into his sister's eyes. Frankie believed Pearl actually might be frightened.

The boy inched over to the edge of his dresser and peered down at the floor, wondering how he was ever going to get off.

"Don't make me come in there, girls," Mr. Keenan said loudly. His words spoke anger, but Frankie heard something else in the voice that he couldn't place. He developed a sudden urge to jump down off the top of the dresser, and crash-landed on his bottom on the floor.

Frankie hopped up to his feet, even though he had a hurt bottom, and burst out of his bedroom door. Father had a hand on the bathroom doorknob. Frankie wrapped his arms around his father's waist and shouted, "Don't go in there, Daddy. Pearl and Francine are taking a bath."

Mr. Keenan slapped an angry expression on his face. "What are you up to, Franklin? What have you been doing, boy? Have you been watching those girls taking a bath?"

"No, sir." Frankie lied without meaning to. It's just that the way his father had put it—"watching those girls taking a bath"—didn't sound exactly like what he had been doing. In a court of law, Frankie would have argued he was watching those girls play a game called baptism. Still in all, he supposed it was a lie, technically speaking.

"DORIS," Mr. Keenan yelled. "Come up here right now and put this boy to bed."

Frankie started to cry despite already being five years old, on account of the unfairness of getting sent to bed, even though he had told a lie. It was one thing to get sent to bed by his father, but it was another thing to get put to bed by his mother, who wasn't any way involved in the situation so far as Frankie could determine.

"Doris!"

By the time his mother hauled herself up the stairs to see what all the hollering was about, Pearl had opened the bathroom door, and she and Francine had exited in their pj's with a green towel wrapped around Pearl's head and a pink towel wrapped around Francine's head. Pearl looked squarely into Frankie's eyes and blinked a thank-you signal, which Frankie was too confused by everything else to imagine what on earth she had to thank him for.

Their father explained the situation to their mother, how Frankie was obviously up to no good, and instructed her to put Frankie to bed immediately without any Friday-night snack of family popcorn, which was a punishment Frankie could tell his mother didn't agree with, but then she didn't make a peep to argue against it either.

Frankie put on his pj's with an attitude of unfairness and hurt, brushed his teeth with more of the same, crawled into bed with another powerful unnamed feeling, and started to cry again when his mother sat down on the edge of his bed to say prayers with him. With so many strong emotions swishing around inside, he went ahead and confessed to her the whole truth, how he'd spied on Pearl and Francine while they were in the bathtub, and he proclaimed between snuffles how very sorry he was to be such a constant sinner.

Mother said he certainly should be sorry, even though it is a good thing to tell the truth and not compound an original sin with lying added on. She also offered the opinion that Father should have fixed the hole in Frankie's bedroom wall before then, and if he had fixed that hole, there wouldn't have been any opportunity for spying into the bathroom.

It took Frankie a long time to fall asleep that night because of being sent to bed so early and also because of the smell of popcorn wafting up the stairs. He cried a little more in the aloneness of his bedroom before stopping and deciding he was too old for that.

After it turned dark, he heard a quiet knock on his bedroom door, but he didn't say, "Come in," in case it was a trick to see whether he was asleep like he should have been.

The door opened, and Pearl snuck in. "Here," she whispered and put a yellow plastic bowl of popcorn on his bed. She left without saying another word and closed the door tightly behind her, which signaled coast is clear for eating the popcorn. Frankie ate it with gratitude and without calculating whether or not eating stolen popcorn constituted another demerit in the Lamb's book of life.

By the time he fell asleep that night, Frankie had forgotten all about his sister getting baptized in the name of Walking Mary. Instead, his thoughts got caught up with a substitute perplexity. Why do girls find taking a bath so much fun, when boys would rather do almost anything else?

Take himself, for example. What Frankie preferred to do, if it was going to be something secretive with a friend that involved water, was to pee-piss his name in the snow. Now *that* was a sport requiring skill, stamina, and legible handwriting. As far as Frankie was concerned, this game had only one drawback. *Frankie* was too long to be a really first-class pee-pissing name. He envied his friend Jim for the obvious benefits of having a short name, though he acknowledged that dotting an *i* presented certain challenges. All things considered, *Sam* would be the perfect name. *Sam* flows.

Three

NOT EVERYTHING THAT HAPPENED to the four Keenans—Mother, Father, Pearl Harbor, and Franklin—during the early 1950s could be laid at the feet of Walking Mary. On the other hand, for those with eyes to see, more things than are in heaven or on earth just *might* have been related to Walking Mary.

After the incident at Veterans' Park and the scene outside the bathroom, Mr. Keenan appeared nearly to drop out of the family portrait. Sure, he continued to get up every morning before sunrise, put on a gray suit and a white shirt with striped tie, and go to the State Bank of Framburg, where he worked as the cashier and number-one loan officer. He came home every night to have supper with the family. And he continued to do the minimum of father things, such as throwing the baseball with Frankie in the backyard, if he absolutely couldn't get out of it. Father was a pillar of the church, called a deacon, and as such expressed himself oddly from time to time. For instance, Mr. Keenan objected when the Framburg Baptist Fellowship evangelization board out in front of the church building carried the following message: "What if the Hokey Pokey really IS what it's all about?" He could spot dancing from around the corner.

Mrs. Keenan was another story, and a sadder one. She took to living either in fear or in fantasy, one or the other, and sometimes both at the same time. She was afraid of almost everybody, especially her husband, whose words and dictates she never contradicted. She exerted herself rarely as a parent, and then only by undergroundedness and slip-sliding along the squeaky edges of her children's lives. Exactly what she was afraid of Frankie did not know, but he could say for absolutely certain that their mother had become Our Lady of Perpetual Afraidness, which was a Catholic way of saying she was skitterish and scaredy-cat-like, and sometimes Frankie enjoyed speaking Catholic in his private imagination.

As to the fantasy part, Mrs. Keenan was a world champion book reader. She read one book each day—one complete book every single day. This meant she entered into a new world, the made-up world of that day's book, every twenty-four hours, and met fifteen or twenty or thirty new characters every twenty-four hours, and lived their lives more or less inside her mind instead of paying full attention to her own life. Add them up, and that's a whole lot of worlds, a whole lot of characters, and a whole lot of imagination. The only time Frankie had ever heard his mother and father argue out loud had to do with all of Mother's reading.

Father had said, "Doris, every book you read changes you."

And Mother had replied, "At least I know how to read, Franklin."

Which had been a low blow as far as Frankie was concerned because his father *did* know how to read. It's just that Father didn't choose to exercise this skill except on *The Framburg File*, their town's daily newspaper, every once in a while. Father maintained that reading was for girls and women, not for boys and men, an idea which Frankie absorbed and agreed with. Besides, Frankie believed there was some truth to the charge that every book his mother read changed her somewhat. At the rate of one book per day, that amounts to extreme changeableness over time. He hated to side with his father, but what else was he supposed to do?

Mother's combination of fear and fantasy also made her fat—very fat. She spent many whole days in her bedroom with the door closed, lying in bed, reading and eating potato chips. On these days, Frankie and Pearl wouldn't see her until suppertime, when she'd appear and make supper for the family before Father got home. Her meals were never tasty or nutritious, but they were quick, which has its own advantages if a boy wants to go outside and play baseball before dark.

In contrast to Mother's getting fatter and fatter, Pearl got thinner and thinner. Instead of eating her food, she would push it around the edges of the plate with her fork or spoon, making geometrical patterns. Mother did not appear to notice this behavior of Pearl's. Frankie considered it favoritism on his mother's part, since he had to concoct many different strategies to avoid swallowing beets or peas from off his own plate. Mother monitored *his* plate but seemed oblivious to Pearl's. Also, Mother did not appear to notice Pearl's appearance. Frankie believed Father *did* notice, because every once in a while he would say something like, "Isn't Pearl getting pretty, Doris?"

As for Frankie, Mr. Keenan accused his son of being a liar, which, strictly speaking, he was, but only on about half the occasions Father accused him of. A distinction needed to be drawn, Frankie believed, between lying proper—which was a sin—and telling interesting stories—which was not, in Frankie's book. This distinction appeared to mean nothing whatever to Father.

Hypothetical Case Number One: Father might ask Frankie if he had brushed his teeth. Maybe Frankie would say, "Yes, sir," when in fact he had not brushed his teeth. This case represents a clear lie, and Frankie's point would have been to avoid punishment for not having brushed his teeth.

Hypothetical Case Number Two: Say there had been a fight among neighborhood boys in somebody's front yard. Father might ask, "What was going on out there, Frankie?" And Frankie would answer truthfully with a blow-by-blow description of the event. Later, perhaps, Mr. Keenan would run into another parent and get a different story. Then he'd accuse Frankie, "You were lying when you told me what was going on out there. It didn't happen the way you said it did at all." In this case, Frankie believed *lying* was an inappropriate word. He had told the story of the boys' fighting to the best of his ability, using all of his considerable imagination. Accuracy is only one virtue when it comes to storytelling, Frankie thought, and it isn't necessarily the highest virtue.

To summarize the Keenans in the 1950s up to 1957, Mother came to live in her own world of fear and fantasy. Father went off to live in his own world at the bank. Pearl lived in her own world too, which was full of truth and grace but contained almost no calories. Finally, Frankie lived in all their other worlds—Mother's, Father's, and Pearl's—which proved exhausting. Mother grew as big as a barn, Pearl shrank as skinny as a weathervane, Father froze up as hard as a slab, and Frankie developed migraine headaches, which stayed with him for many years to come.

THERE WAS ONE OTHER SIGNIFICANT encounter between Pearl and Walking Mary before 1957. Frankie was not present to witness it, but Pearl told him about it later. This episode took place when Pearl was thirteen years old and in the eighth grade. Pearl was still friends with Francine, and the two of them had a third friend named Suzie Fortinelli. Toward the end of their spring vacation, on Good Friday, all three girls felt bored and were looking for adventure. Suzie phoned up the other two to suggest coloring Easter eggs at her house, and they decided to meet at the Piggly-Wiggly grocery store. In the dairy aisle, the girls spotted cardboard cartons containing eighteen eggs each, on sale. As Pearl told it to Frankie, she could not recall which of them had come up with the idea of *throwing* those eggs instead of coloring them. Whatever the reason, they found themselves with an afternoon to kill and fifty-four eggs with which to kill it.

Francine believed they might discover something interesting by way of a target in the neighborhood of Louise Fishback's house. Suzie agreed, and Pearl completed their plot by supplying a street name. Since the fourth grade, Louise had graduated from squishing peanut butter and jelly through her teeth to belching on cue and bragging about her size-C cups. Neither talent immunized her house against an egg attack.

Francine rationalized, "We wouldn't hit a window or anything like that."

Suzie recommended a tree in the front yard as the best target.

Pearl favored the Fishbacks' garage door as the greater challenge. "We'd have to sneak up close to hit it and then peel out of there if anybody spots us."

"Kids' stuff," Francine concluded.

They located Louise's house, heaved the first few eggs from behind a high hedge, and then took turns running out into the open driveway for a frontal assault on the garage. In total, they splattered six eggs against the garage

door, resulting in good overall coverage. Then they made a clean getaway, still in possession of forty-eight eggs ready for firing.

A couple of blocks away, they took aim at Lincoln Elementary, their old grade school. Since today was a holiday, they could count on no teachers snooping around. The only children likely to use the playground would be much younger and easy to scare off if worse came to worst. After some serious debate, they agreed on an entrance to the building right next to the swing sets and teeter-totters as their best target. This school was ancient. Francine's mother had gone there umpteen years before, back when boys and girls had to line up at different doors to go into class every morning. Above the playground door were letters carved into a concrete slab permanently marking this old-fashioned tradition: BOYS ENTRANCE. The girls decided to aim their eggs smack at such stupidity.

This new gambit demanded greater skill, as well as more courage, than the Fishback venture. Here they had to stand out in the open, with traffic flowing by in both directions on Stephenson Street, to have any reasonable chance of hitting the target.

The girls decided to throw four eggs apiece. Whoever cracked the most eggs against the Boys Entrance sign would

win, and the winner would get to choose their next point of attack. In case of a tie, there'd be a two-egg shoot-off.

As things turned out, no need to worry about ties. Francine splatted all four of her eggs in the target area, while Pearl could only hit with two, and Suzie succeeded in a measly one out of four. Actually, the misses proved more interesting than the hits. All the misses struck low, smacking hard against the metal doorframe and dripping yellow egg yolks, mixed with bits of shell in sticky whites, down the length of the school's glass doors.

On Suzie's final throw, two little boys (they looked like third graders) came running onto the playground shouting, "Hey, what are you doing?"

Francine hollered, "Give it to 'em," and all three girls let loose simultaneously with well-aimed eggs. They'd never seen two kids hit the brakes, throw it into reverse, and skedaddle faster than those boys did.

"That'll teach 'em to mess with their superiors," Suzie declared.

"Eggheads!" Francine yelled after them, just for effect.

Pearl called a conference to count their remaining assets. After twelve eggs spent on the Lincoln School competition and three more unloaded against the boys, they had thirty-three eggs to go. The girls wasted nine of these

trying to hit a streetlamp, which was the winner's chosen target. Next, Suzie came up with the bright idea of egging the Framburg Baptist Fellowship, but Pearl vetoed this on account of being a member. Then they all figured it wouldn't be too blasphemous to decorate the red doors of St. Margaret's, since none of them happened to be Episcopalian.

That left eighteen eggs, and no one could determine what victim should come next after the church. Their ammo supply was getting low, and they didn't want to waste any eggs on an unworthy target. Pearl, Francine, and Suzie strolled toward downtown Framburg, each armed with an eighteen-egg carton one third full. None of them was fool enough to suggest egging a storefront. Their fates were sealed when Pearl suggested scouting out the train station.

Every weekday afternoon at precisely 4:07, the Land O' Corn pulled into the Framburg depot on its way from Chicago to Des Moines, Kansas City, and points farther west. When the girls walked past the Sizzle Shop, just two blocks from the railroad tracks, they heard a distant whistle announcing the train's approach.

Pearl sang out, "Train's a-coming," to the tune of some old TV western.

"Train's a-coming," Suzie echoed.

"A train's coming?" Francine asked, drawling out her words. "A train's coming, you say?"

All three of them started walking faster. "I hope you're not thinking what I think you're thinking," Pearl said.

Francine broke into a slow trot, and the other two followed in stride. "What do you think I'm thinking?" Francine asked.

"You're not thinking of egging a train, are you?"

"Why, Pearl Keenan, what a horrible idea. I wish I'd thought of it myself."

"You did."

"Not me. You're the one with the evil mind."

Suzie cautioned, "It's against the law, isn't it?"

"What is?" Pearl asked.

"To egg a train."

"Only if you get caught," Francine said, laughing.

With one block to go, they accelerated into a run. The Land O' Corn blew its whistle again, and the bells of the warning gates began to clang.

"Hurry," Francine shouted.

The depot stood on the other side, where a small crowd of people were already gathered on the platform to welcome the train. The girls were too late to cross over. They'd conduct their attack from the train's blind side. As Pearl ran for the shelter of a wooden baggage cart, she spotted Walking Mary standing apart from the assembly. As usual, the old lady was wrapped in her worn mink coat and carrying an umbrella. Because she was so short, Walking Mary was already looking upward, prepared to inspect each passing window as the train pulled in.

While concentrating on the business at hand, none of the girls gave a thought to Walking Mary, although, if asked, each of them would have been familiar with her routine. Every child and adult in town knew that the old lady met every single passenger train that pulled into Framburg— morning, noon, and night, seven days a week, including holidays. With each arrival, she would walk rapidly along the platform, first on one side of the coaches and then, crossing behind the caboose, along the other side. She would inspect every single window, probably appearing to the passengers inside the train like some ghostly character out of a scary old movie.

The train's whistle blew long and loud as a line of heavy cars straightened into view. The Land O' Corn presented one beautiful sight to all Framburgers, a gold-and-green dream machine connecting their little town to the rest of the mighty world.

Francine tried to shout over the throbbing racket of the locomotive, but the other girls couldn't catch every single word. "Double for moving . . . !"

The three girls came to a stop beside the baggage wagon. They set their cardboard cartons on top of its wooden deck and popped open the lids, picking out as many eggs as each could hold in one hand.

Suzie shouted, "What if somebody sees us?"

"Then it's every man for himself," Francine called back.

Pearl elbowed her. "You mean every girl for herself."

"Quick," Francine commanded, "hit it while it's moving." She hurled an egg in the direction of the train, but it fell short.

The Land O' Corn pulled only five cars that day. Usually a mail car would come first after the locomotive, but the mail car was missing, leaving a baggage car in the lead. Then followed the diner, two passenger coaches, and the caboose.

Suzie's first throw, like Francine's, didn't reach its mark. Then Pearl splattered the door of the baggage car as it rolled past. Francine screamed her congratulations. "Bull's-eye!"

The train heaved to a stop. Smoke and steam spewed out from under the cars, issuing from valves and hoses and other parts unknown. The engine was still noisy but not as loud as when it was in motion. The bells at the safety gates clanged. With the assistance of conductors, passengers disembarked onto the platform.

Suzie and Francine had luck with their next throws, cracking eggs against the wheels of the second passenger coach. Pearl hit a window dead center, but no one was sitting on the inside of it.

Now the locomotive blew its whistle, eager to depart. Pearl had her sights fixed on a caboose window as the grand prize for egging a train. She took careful aim, pumped up her arm for a power throw, and then let loose with an arching beauty. As the egg flew through the air, with Pearl marveling at its perfect arc, two other moving points converged unseen. First, the caboose man settled back into his seat and glanced out the window. Second, Walking Mary stepped from behind the train in the middle of her rapid round of inspection.

Pearl's egg missed the caboose man's window, but the caboose man didn't miss it. Just below his window, he watched the egg strike Walking Mary square on her forehead. All three girls saw the egg hit its mark. Suzie ran away without a word of farewell. Francine shouted, "You're in trouble," and took off after Suzie. Only Pearl was left standing there, staring in stunned silence as Walking Mary flinched momentarily and jerked her head instinctively in the direction from which she'd been struck.

Pearl could not say whether the old lady had spotted her. She couldn't even say whether Walking Mary knew what had hit her. Walking Mary didn't stop to wipe off the egg, but her wrinkled face winced as she looked up into each passenger's window, continuing her brisk tour.

Immediately, Pearl regretted throwing that egg. All in a rush, she wished she hadn't thrown any eggs on that day. Her stomach tightened into a rotten ache as she watched Walking Mary proceed the length of the train.

The caboose man opened his window and began shouting at Pearl, shaking his fist. Instead of running away, Pearl took a few steps toward the train. She might have made it all the way to Walking Mary's side if Francine hadn't returned to the scene of the crime, grabbed her friend from behind, twisted Pearl around, and shoved her in the opposite direction, hard.

"Are you crazy, girl?" Francine shouted into her ear. "They'll catch us all. Follow me."

Fright took command of Pearl's legs, and she fled with Francine, abandoning what eggs remained as evidence of their Good Friday folly. Except for Francine's protective maneuver, Pearl might have gone right up to Walking Mary and met her face-to-face at age thirteen. As things turned out, that meeting would have to wait for another three and a half years.

Four

M RS. KEENAN COULD SCRAMBLE eggs two different
ways. The first was runny like a river and yellow like
a . . . like an uncooked egg. The second was hard like a rock
and brown like a . . . a burnt egg. On November 2, 1957—
two days after Halloween—she had opted for Scrambled
Eggs Number One, the runny kind, and spooned up gener-
ous helpings onto all four plates. After Mr. Keenan prayed
for God to bless the eggs to everyone's nourishment, as well
as to help the United States surpass the Russians in the space
race, he took a large bite of his scrambled eggs. Mrs.
Keenan, who now weighed more than two hundred pounds,
smiled at everyone around the table and announced that
she wasn't hungry on account of a "diminished appetite."
Frankie—age fourteen by then—closed his eyes before
taking a test bite. If he were asked to declare a preference in
the matter of his mother's scrambled eggs, Frankie definitely

preferred the hard and brown ones to the runny and yellow ones because the hard and brown ones went down quicker. However, he had never been asked to state a preference and, to tell the truth, he came close to gagging on both styles.

On any ordinary morning, Pearl would have started pushing the runny eggs around her plate instead of eating them. But November 2, 1957—just five weeks shy of her sixteenth birthday—would not turn out to be an ordinary Saturday for Pearl Keenan. While reaching for her fork, Pearl suddenly fainted facedown in her plate of scrambled eggs.

This fainting episode, the first of its kind in their family, caused an enormous stir.

Mother shouted, "Pearl!" like Pearl had fainted on purpose.

Father reached a hand over the table toward Pearl's head, which was facedown in the middle of her plate.

Frankie hollered, "Pull her up. Pull her up. She's gonna drown."

Father pulled Pearl's face out of the gooey mess, which provoked her mother to say, "Oh, for goodness' sake, would you look at that," in a voice full of distaste.

Father tried to wipe off the egg with a napkin, but Pearl's head kept flipping this way and that, and the task proved too difficult for him. Next, he laid Pearl down on the kitchen floor—she didn't weigh hardly a thing—and got a towel from the counter to do the job proper.

Mother spoke up again: "Oh, for crying out loud."

"Slap her," Frankie suggested, helpfully. He was worried to death about his sister, and he had seen this extreme measure on a TV show about life-and-death rescues.

Mother pulled Pearl's plate over and spooned its remaining contents onto her own plate. "No sense wasting food," Mother said, and she began to eat the runny scrambled eggs with relish, like they were chocolate pudding or something. Then she nodded sternly at Frankie. "Enough foolishness. You eat up too, young man."

Pearl rolled her eyes and groaned. Frankie thought her nonsense noises came straight from la-la land.

Then Father left to carry Pearl upstairs.

"I've lost my appetite," Frankie said, pushing his chair back from the table. "But they sure were delicious eggs, Mother."

Mother paused before answering, stabbing another mouthful with her fork. "Really?"

"I think they're your best," Frankie declared.

"Well, it wasn't the eggs," Mother said with conviction. "Your sister has a bug, that's all."

"I know it wasn't the eggs," Frankie agreed, standing

up. "That's for sure."

"Where are you going, honey?"

"Upstairs to check on Pearl."

"Father can handle her, Frankie. Your father always prefers to handle your sister alone."

"I know that," Frankie said, remembering how Father used to prefer handling Pearl alone but, for a few years now, hadn't paid her much attention at all. The boy exited the kitchen in a hurry.

Up on the second story, the door to Pearl's bedroom was closed. Frankie stood outside it but couldn't hear anything. He turned the handle, pushed open the door, and walked in.

Pearl lay on her back in the bed, and Father lay beside her, rubbing her stomach with his hand. Pearl's eyes were open, staring at Frankie.

"How you feeling?"

"I've got the situation under control, son," Father said. "You go back downstairs with your mother."

"Pearl, do *you* want me to go back downstairs?"

She shook her head slightly, no.

"Go on now, Frankie," Father urged.

"I think not, sir," Frankie said.

"What did you say?"

"I said, I think I'll stay here with Pearl, sir."

Mr. Keenan rolled over to the edge of the bed, stood up, and took a couple of steps toward Frankie. "Get downstairs with your mother like I said, and stay down there unless I call for you."

Frankie looked over at Pearl, who stared at him for a moment, then closed her eyes.

"I know what's best for your sister," Father said. "You get downstairs now."

Frankie about-faced and left the room. Father stretched out his foot and kicked the door closed behind him.

The boy went to his own bedroom, grabbed his twenty-seven-inch Louisville Slugger with Ernie Banks's autograph on it, and marched straight back into Pearl's room.

Father stared up at Frankie, startled. "Why do you have your baseball bat?"

"Now *you* go back downstairs with Mother," Frankie said, gripping the bat with both hands.

Father was too surprised to speak.

Pearl whispered, "Please, Daddy. Go downstairs. I'm fine now. Frankie can stay with me."

As Father inched past Frankie, he gave his son a threatening look, as if to say, "You wouldn't dare."

The boy gripped his baseball bat tighter, wishing it were

a hatchet. He stepped aside and let Father walk out of the room.

"Come over here," Pearl said weakly.

Frankie walked around the side of his sister's bed and sat down on the floor. He kept hold of the bat.

"You're crazy," Pearl whispered.

"Maybe."

"You wouldn't have hit him, would you?"

"What happened downstairs?" he asked Pearl.

"I fainted."

"I know. I was there. I mean, *why* did you faint?"

"Too hungry, I suppose."

"Too hungry for Mother's eggs? I don't think so."

"And something else, too, maybe," she admitted.

"Like what?"

"I was thinking about something that happened on Halloween while I was at work at CBB."

CBB is short for Calvary Bible Bookstore, which is on Lincoln Boulevard in downtown Framburg, right next to the Buff & Puff shoeshine and cigar stand, and just before you reach the railroad tracks. Pearl worked there stocking shelves with maps of the Holy Land, puppet prophets of the Old Testament, and stacks of flash cards filled with Sacred Stumpers.

"What happened?" Frankie asked.

"I don't know if I should tell you," Pearl said, closing her eyes.

"Come on, you can tell me anything."

Still with her eyes closed, "Not everything."

Frankie set the baseball bat on the floor and crossed his legs, waiting.

"You know what, Frankie?" Pearl asked dreamily, keeping her eyes shut.

"What?"

Instead of telling Frankie the secret he suspected, the secret he might already have guessed when he went to get his baseball bat, she said, "I believe I'd prefer to be a colored girl rather than a white girl."

"A Negro?"

"In fact, I'm sure I'd prefer to be a colored girl."

Frankie saw a pinch of pink come back into his sister's cheeks, and he took this as a good sign.

Although Pearl was in the middle of talking, she closed her eyes and, it appeared to Frankie, fell asleep. Ordinarily, he would have prompted her to go on, but that morning he was content to let Pearl set the pace for their conversation. Whatever his sister was going through, he could tell she was exhausted. When she finally opened her eyes—maybe ten minutes later—Pearl did not continue with her explanation for wanting to become a Negro. Instead, she went right on telling the events of the evening before last, as if there had been no interruption.

"I was standing at the window of CBB watching the trick-or-treaters come and go," she said.

Many shops in downtown Framburg stayed open on Halloween for trick-or-treaters. The best one was the Emerald Emporium, with its bowls and jars of penny candy. You could take any three pieces you wanted for free on Halloween night, in exchange for giving one kiss to Ruby, who worked behind the counter. When Frankie was very young, he considered this a reasonable exchange. As he grew older, however, the bargain began to feel costlier and costlier until he decided to bypass the Emerald Emporium, thereby losing three pieces of penny candy, which would have been very delicious, especially if they happened to be malted milk balls, but also avoiding having to kiss Ruby.

The Calvary Bible Bookstore, on the other hand, distributed to trick-or-treaters what its owner, Brother Terry, called Christian Candy Cards. They were little plastic cards with an edifying painting on one side—say, of our Lord chasing the money changers out of the temple—and an edifying saying on the other side—maybe, "Jesus outfoxes

Satan every time. Have a sanctified Halloween." Scotch-taped onto the card was one stick of black licorice to remind boys and girls that they were sinners and going directly to hell if they didn't straighten up and fly right. Pearl's job was to pass out Christian Candy Cards to any trick-or-treater who entered the store, although many children didn't like to go into the Calvary Bible Bookstore, preferring the Buff & Puff next door, where they were allowed to select a bubble-gum cigar out of a genuine-looking cigar box. Frankie had always wanted to go into the Buff & Puff himself but was forbidden to enter by the *Baptist Fellowship Statement of Faith Practices and Policies*. He envied his friends these devilish delicacies—pink, green, and yellow cigars—and vowed he would smoke a real cigar, an actual cigar, if he should ever get kicked out of the Baptist Fellowship for any reason in the future.

"There was this rowdy group of boys, four of them, who walked up and down Lincoln Boulevard all night long," Pearl reported. "I recognized Ronnie Shasker, but I couldn't tell who any of the others were for certain. They were wearing costumes with masks, although they were too old to be trick-or-treating."

"Shasker's a shyster," Frankie added, not knowing the exact meaning of the word *shyster* but liking the feel, the sound, of *Shasker's a shyster* as a made-up, English-language phrase.

"At first, they kept walking by CBB and just looking in our window. They'd sneer like they were too good to come into a Bible bookstore, and that was okay by me."

Frankie said, "They'd just throw away Brother Terry's Christian Candy Cards anyway. You know they would."

"Also, Walking Mary passed by the store more than once through the evening."

"Walking Mary? Why?"

"You know how she walks around downtown between trains. Halloween is the same for her as any other evening, I guess."

Frankie tried to imagine Walking Mary mingling with trick-or-treaters on Lincoln Boulevard. Halloween might be the only night of the year when she *wouldn't* appear strange. Her usual getup—mink coat, umbrella, and old-fashioned high-heeled shoes—could easily be mistaken for the costume of some down-on-her-luck Hollywood actress. Could easily be mistaken, except that Walking Mary was a Negro, a fact that Frankie did not associate with Hollywood actresses because movie stars back then were almost all white.

"About nine thirty—I had just checked the clock because

I wanted to close up—I saw Walking Mary go past the window one more time, and those four boys were following right behind her, close. They were laughing at her, I could tell."

"At Walking Mary?"

"And then, just past the Buff and Puff, they ran up and circled around her on the sidewalk."

"How do you know?"

"I stepped out the front door of the store and watched. Something told me there was going to be trouble."

"And was there?"

"They made a circle around her, and one of them said, 'Where you going, lady?'"

"They actually talked to Walking Mary?"

"Since it was four against one, and they had her surrounded, they must have felt brave enough to bully her."

Frankie exhaled a simple "sheez," trying not to imagine the evil spell Walking Mary could visit on each of those boys if she chose to.

"Then one of them—it was Ronnie—reached out and shoved her on the arm. Shoved her hard."

"Shoved Walking Mary?"

"Another boy asked with his voice all mocking, 'Who touched you, Mary? If you're a witch, tell us who it was who touched you.' The other boys started laughing."

Frankie let out another "sheez," glad he hadn't been there, feeling creepy just hearing about it.

"She didn't answer. She didn't say a single word. She just took a couple steps forward. That's when all four boys locked arms and wouldn't let her out of their circle. They closed the circle in, tighter and tighter, and then began pushing and shoving Walking Mary one way and another, like they were the spinning tub in an automatic washing machine. She lost her balance and stumbled."

"Where were you then?"

"By then, I'd taken a couple steps toward them, but I was still in front of the bookstore window. Frankie, I should have gone right over there and chased those boys away from her, but I was too scared."

"They would have gotten you, too. There was nothing you could do."

"I don't know about that. I should have tried, at least."

Frankie shook his head. He knew what Pearl was feeling, but he would never have had the courage to take on four boys at the same time, especially if one of them was Ronnie Shasker, and especially if the person they were picking on was Walking Mary.

"They started spinning around faster and faster,

bumping into her as they spun. Finally, she fell down on the sidewalk, and I could see her arm was bleeding."

"She didn't hit them with her umbrella or cast any spell on them?"

"No. She stood perfectly still and took it. They knocked her down and then just stared at her."

One more "sheez" of utter disbelief from Frankie.

"That's when two Negro children—one boy and one girl, dressed as Raggedy Ann and Andy—came charging out of Buff and Puff. They shouted and screamed like they were Indians on a warpath, running straight at those four boys. They were smaller and younger than the four boys, but they didn't care."

Frankie couldn't speak. This story wasn't going to end well, he could tell.

"The colored kids hollered, 'Let her go, let her go,' and busted right through the circle of arms surrounding Walking Mary. I don't think the boys knew what to do. Ronnie threatened, 'You're in *big* trouble, I can tell you. *Big* trouble.' Still, the boys let loose their arms and backed away from Walking Mary, almost like they were afraid. 'We're going to find a policeman,' Ronnie said. 'Then we'll see who's so tough.'"

"What about Walking Mary?" Frankie asked.

"She sat slumped on the ground and didn't move. She

didn't even rub her arm where it was scratched."

"Was she hurt bad?"

"The two colored children knelt down beside her and hugged her around the shoulders. Raggedy Andy wiped the blood on her arm with his hand."

"Hugged Walking Mary?" Frankie could hardly believe this.

"Yep. They were hugging her, showing so much more courage than me, and I started walking toward them."

"Where did Ronnie and the other boys go to?"

"They ran across the street, saying, 'Police, police,' but not very loud. Not like they meant it."

"Sheez."

"When I got close enough, I could hear the little children asking Walking Mary, 'Are you all right, Mama? Did they hurt you, Mama?'"

"They called her 'Mama'?"

"Not only that, Frankie, but they put their hands under her arms and lifted her to her feet. 'Come on, Mama,' they said. 'Let's get you out of here.'"

"Wow."

"By then I'd walked right up to where they were. Walking Mary turned around and looked me straight in the eye."

"Scary."

"No, Frankie, that's the strange thing. It wasn't scary at all. She just smiled at me, even though I knew she had to be in pain. Then, quick as anything, she reached out and whacked me a good one with her umbrella right on the shin."

"What?"

Pearl reached down and rubbed her right leg where Walking Mary had struck her. "It wasn't that hard."

"She hit you?"

"And then she just turned around and walked off toward the train station with those two little children, one on each side of her. It was amazing."

"What did you do?"

"I stood there for a little while in case the police actually came, which I thought they wouldn't because Ronnie and his friends would have been afraid to tell the whole truth of what happened."

"Did they come?"

"Never."

"Whew."

"But I'll tell you something, Frankie. Walking Mary was lucky those little kids came out to rescue her. Who knows what would have happened. She's so old and frail.

Those boys could have hurt her bad. Or worse."

"No wonder you were still scared at breakfast."

But that's not what Pearl was thinking about. "I just stood there, Frankie. They could have killed her, and I didn't do a thing. I was too frightened."

Frankie nodded his head.

Pearl laid her head back on the pillow and closed her eyes. "Thanks, Frankie, for saving me this morning. That took courage like crazy."

"Saving you from what?" he asked.

But Pearl was not listening. Either that, or she preferred not to answer. "Yes, I'm sure of it," his sister said, her eyes still closed. "I'd like to be a colored girl."

FRANKIE DID NOT KNOW what to make of Pearl's desire to become a Negro, but he did know how to interpret the news he heard in school the next Monday morning. Ronnie Shasker and three other boys had developed boils all over their bodies, a condition well known to Baptists because of Old Testament pestilences dealt out by an angry God against sinners of one kind and another. The high-school principal announced that all four boys must have drunk contaminated water somehow, and the rest of the children should let this be a lesson to them all.

However, Frankie knew those boils on the boys had to be the direct result of their messing with Walking Mary. He believed they should count themselves lucky to get away with boils instead of a major pestilence such as having their firstborns killed by the Angel of Death. Walking Mary could have chosen that one just as easily, and then where would they be?

Five

AFTER THAT HALLOWEEN NIGHT, it was as if Pearl was on a mission to get to know everything she possibly could about Walking Mary. Her search started the following Monday when she ditched seventh-period chemistry—her first cut ever—and walked from Framburg High downtown to the train station. The walk took about a half hour and put her at the depot around 3:15. The Land O' Corn wasn't due to arrive until 4:07.

Pearl's route directed her down Empire Street as far as the Second Presbyterian Church and then left onto River Drive. Houses stood on only one side of River Drive, with the railroad tracks taking up the other side and then, farther east, the river itself, which is called the Pecatonica and used to carry barge traffic. Pearl and Frankie, along with most everybody else in Framburg, skated on the Pecatonica River during the coldest months of winter, clear from the Sturgess

Battery Company, past the Twin Caves, behind the athletic field of St. Felicity, all the way to Veterans' Park.

Pearl's main concern on that day was to catch sight of Walking Mary before Walking Mary caught sight of her, which meant finding a position somewhere near the station for the purpose of observing.

Standing on River Drive, across the street from the railroad tracks, Pearl looked carefully at the depot. It appeared strange, on account of Pearl's never having approached the old building from this side before. She could see a small door at the end of the depot reserved for station workers. Two men stacked some brown parcels and hefted a canvas mail pouch onto a baggage cart just outside the main door of the station. Lights were on inside the building, and a few automobiles were parked behind it, which suggested there were people inside waiting for the train to come, but nobody except those two workers had walked out onto the platform yet.

When Pearl spotted Walking Mary crossing the tracks on Lincoln Boulevard and heading for the station, she scurried for cover behind an elm tree. Pearl watched Walking Mary cross the tracks, turn south, and proceed along the platform toward the depot, observing her all the way until Walking Mary went inside.

Then Pearl dashed across River Drive to the railroad tracks, ran through the tall grass onto the gravel rail bed, skipped over the low hurdles of the track itself, and made a run for the underbrush on the far side toward an evergreen tree, maybe eight feet tall and four feet around, twenty yards from the end of the platform, where she could hide. At four o'clock, people began coming out of the station to wait for the train on the platform. The Land O' Corn ran like clockwork back then, rarely arriving early and never arriving late.

When Walking Mary joined the small crowd outside, she made her way toward the far end of the platform. She was so short and slight that she almost disappeared among taller, bulkier folks, and Pearl had to keep a sharp eye on her. Pearl figured Walking Mary would begin her inspection tour on the near side of the train, cross behind the caboose, and then make her way toward the locomotive on the far side, just as she had always done, three times each day, every single day, for nearly forty years. Just as Walking Mary had done that unfortunate Good Friday when Pearl threw an Easter egg and hit Walking Mary in the head, for which act Pearl would never forgive herself even if God Almighty might, someday.

A whistle sounded, the train came into view, the bells on

the warning gates started to clang, and everybody waiting on the platform tensed into stillness. When the Land O' Corn stopped, Pearl observed Walking Mary go through her inspection routine, the same as every other day, with the same results, which is to say no results whatever. Nothing. The engineer blew a short whistle just as Walking Mary rounded the front edge of the locomotive, stepped slowly over both rails, and hoisted herself back onto the platform. The engineer leaned out his window and checked to make sure she was clear of the tracks before sounding his whistle one last time and setting the Land O' Corn into motion. Pearl was so focused on Walking Mary that it startled her to feel how close the train passed by, gathering speed in its departure from Framburg. The man in the caboose noticed her standing behind the pine tree and gave a friendly wave.

Pearl was glad when the train had moved on. Its power and weight felt too close for comfort. When she looked back toward the station again, Walking Mary stood alone on the platform. Pearl stepped out from behind the pine tree and started walking toward the depot.

With each noisy stride, Pearl expected Walking Mary to turn around and see her. But the old woman did not turn around. As she approached closer, Pearl studied the way

Walking Mary's fur coat rested on her thin shoulders, the wiry coarseness of her gray hair sticking out from under a black hat, and the stitchery of her old-fashioned stockings bunched above the heels of her solid black shoes.

Pearl paused at the edge of the platform. She'd never been so close to Walking Mary before, not more than four feet away, except for on that day at the duck pond so many years before, and except for three nights earlier outside the Calvary Bible Bookstore. Still, the old lady stood staring in the other direction and did not move.

The platform came to a height just below Pearl's waist. Had it been a foot shorter, she could have taken a high step onto it. Instead, she had to place both hands onto the edge and boost herself up. Then she stood behind Walking Mary. One step forward, and Pearl could have reached out and touched the woman's mink coat.

Pearl felt butterflies flitting around inside her, zigzagging from behind her knees and up to her throat, as she reached out to touch the untouchable. She had no idea what Walking Mary might be feeling at that moment. Was she tired? Did she want to sit down? Was she just beginning to take in the fact that her only son, once again, had not returned on the Land O' Corn?

Pearl was startled when Walking Mary slowly turned

around, reached out, and took both the girl's hands into hers. It was Walking Mary who had been waiting for Pearl Keenan to approach, not the other way around.

WAY BACK IN 1957, all citizens of Framburg *thought* they knew who Walking Mary was. Their conventional wisdom was what Pearl would have learned as a little girl, what Frankie would have been taught as a little boy, and what both Mr. and Mrs. Keenan would have passed on to their children. No one possessed any real facts about the town's most mysterious resident. However, stories and rumors got repeated so often over the years that they substituted for facts.

Explanations of who Walking Mary was changed as a child grew older in Framburg. The earliest picture was likely to be of an old colored woman, dressed peculiar, who walked nonstop around the town but never spoke a word. Never. Mean and cranky, she would hit children with her umbrella, or else trip them with it and make them fall.

By age eight or nine, a child probably signed on to the belief that Walking Mary was a witch. This knowledge was supported by many scary stories passed from one child to another. In some of these tales, Walking Mary could fly. In others, she spoke to animals or transformed herself into an alley cat or a thorn tree. In all versions, Walking Mary could cast spells.

By junior high school, a person felt way too grown-up to be scared by witches, goblins, or ghosts. Seventh and eighth graders pretended not to care about Walking Mary at all. At least, that's what they said to one another.

In high school, Mr. Finch's psychology class taught some new vocabulary for theorizing about Framburg's resident crazy woman. Words such as *psychotic, schizophrenic,* and *catatonic* worked like charms to ward off childhood nightmares. They explained things, sort of.

Those high-school graduates who went off to college could forget about Walking Mary for a while. But every trip home would remind them again. Once these college grads moved back to Framburg and started their own families, the learning cycle would begin all over. They taught their children Framburg's one rule of public safety: Never look Walking Mary straight in the eye!

There existed a more-or-less official version of Walking Mary's biography. However, it was impossible to verify the truth of it because no one had ever interviewed Walking Mary, and there were no documents to connect her to neighbor or kin.

The official version held that Walking Mary had a son who

was a soldier in World War I. He was either killed overseas or missing in action, perhaps somewhere in France. Always believing that her son would come back home, Walking Mary dressed up in her finest clothes, put on her mink coat, and met every single train that pulled into town. She would peer hopefully into each coach window, expecting to see him. When her son didn't appear on the 6:14 A.M. train, she'd spend the daytime hours walking along downtown streets, going into various shops but never buying a thing. In the late afternoon, when the 4:07 came through, she'd repeat her faithful inspection. A final passenger service, the California Zephyr, stopped in Framburg at one minute past midnight, and it would find her walking the platform once again.

This more-or-less official explanation carried the day. Details might vary from one telling to the next. Sometimes Walking Mary's son would become a soldier in World War II instead of World War I, although old-timers in Framburg calculated that the woman had been meeting trains long before 1941, so World War II didn't make any sense if you knew your history. Other versions would substitute *husband* for *son*, but these didn't catch on. It was her son's return Mary was waiting for.

Whether you bought the portrait of a cranky old lady,

the image of an evil witch, the diagnosis of a psychotic case, or this official bio, "Keep your distance" remained a pretty good rule. Like their mother always told Pearl and Frankie, "Walking Mary won't hurt you, if you don't hurt her." Or, as their father said, "I'm not saying Walking Mary is of the Devil, in league with certain Dark Dominions and Powers. I'm just saying that our *Baptist Fellowship Statement of Faith Practices and Policies* provides no clear guidance on the matter, so why take chances?"

THE WALKING MARY who turned and grasped Pearl Keenan's hands on the train platform in 1957 did not appear as the dark figure of myth, nor the old lady of rumor, nor the witch of countless children's imaginations. This Walking Mary, who reached out and touched Frankie's sister, was the very person Negro children on Halloween night had called "Mama."

Mother Mary.

At least, that's what Frankie came to believe.

PEARL'S INVESTIGATION of Walking Mary proceeded slowly. She began by going to the train station every day, immediately after school—she could make it to the 4:07 without cutting chemistry again—and trying to wriggle her imagination inside the old lady's skin. Pearl thought maybe she could locate a relative of Mary's, somebody who would know the story for real, although who could say whether Walking Mary had any relatives in the first place? At a minimum, Pearl wanted to find out where Walking Mary lived.

So she walked every day to the train station in time to observe the 4:07, arriving a few minutes before the Land O' Corn, and in time to spot people gathering on the platform, sometimes huddling close together for warmth. Walking Mary did not huddle with anyone else. Instead, she stood by herself, as if oblivious to cold or wind.

In the weeks leading up to Thanksgiving 1957, Pearl hid herself from view until all the other folks had cleared off the platform. Then she watched Walking Mary begin a slow retreat back toward the downtown shopping district. If Walking Mary knew Pearl was close by, she didn't give any sign of it as she had on that first occasion.

Every day, from her secret lookout, Pearl observed Walking Mary. She began to notice small things about the way the old lady waited for a train, the way she inspected that train, and the way she acted after the train's departure. For example, when Walking Mary came out of the station and onto the platform, she would raise her left hand up to the side of her head and make a brushing motion two or three times front to back. Not quite like she was trying to tuck in stray hairs, but more like she was brushing away a cobweb—routine and airy like that. Pearl noticed this detail on about the third or fourth day she went to the station, and then saw Walking Mary do the exact same thing the next day and the days after that.

Another repeated gesture was when Walking Mary would reach down and tap the back of her legs, first the left leg and then the right leg, at the top of her calves and employing the opposite hand from what she had used for wiping away the cobweb. Again, this movement was a small thing which, for several days, Pearl didn't even make a note of. She merely observed that Walking Mary, after clearing away the imaginary cobwebs, would switch the hand in which she held her umbrella. Pearl had thought that *this* gesture was somehow significant. But then she realized the umbrella switching was just a prelude to the genuine item, which was the tap of the back of each leg, first the left and then the right. Pearl catalogued the leg-tapping as another distinctive gesture but couldn't calculate its meaning for a considerable time.

As she made these observations, Pearl began to feel like one of those animal scientists Mr. Finch was always talking about in their psychology class—the ones who live out in the wild jungle in order to record every little movement of some wolf or gorilla. Mr. Finch taught that human beings were animals, too, displaying predictable behaviors, although Pearl's father decided Mr. Finch must not be a Christian and probably shouldn't be allowed to teach at Framburg High, given such ideas.

Walking Mary exhibited other patterned behaviors, too. Pearl wondered whether she was marking her territory as she circled the train, the way a dog will. Was she stalking some prey as she peered into each window, the way a big cat might? These ideas sounded silly, but who could know? That's what Pearl was there to find out. She was there to watch, to listen, and to think about what she was seeing and hearing, in order to understand something more about Walking Mary than anybody else in Framburg cared to discover.

As weeks passed, Pearl grew bolder and bolder, or else more and more careless, and stopped worrying so much about keeping herself hidden. As she had only once before, on her first visit to the station in November, Pearl started stepping out into the open after a train left the station, to observe Walking Mary exiting the platform. When the old lady reached the intersection and turned left onto Lincoln, Pearl climbed up onto the platform and trailed along behind. That gave Walking Mary about a two-block lead, so Pearl figured she was following from a safe distance. Sometimes Pearl would follow Walking Mary all the way to the courthouse before the old lady crossed the street and reversed directions, leaving Pearl to continue walking on ahead, toward the old cemetery, down Burchard Avenue, and safely home to her own house.

If supper wasn't on the table yet, when Pearl arrived home, she'd go straight to her bedroom, close the door, and pull out a notebook she kept hidden between the mattress and box springs, where she wrote down her scientific observations. She recorded Walking Mary's routine movements, as well as any departures from the routine, noting if she stood longer than normal on the platform after a train pulled out, making mention of a cough or any change in the regular pace of walking, as well as many other details. Pearl kept exact records of when Walking Mary arrived at the station and when she left, noting where Walking Mary went after the train. The girl conducted her investigation every school day, come rain or shine, and on any Saturday when she could make a plausible excuse for getting away from the house.

CHRISTMAS EVE 1957, Pearl and Frankie were sitting together on the floor of his bedroom, playing a game of

Monopoly. Both were good Monopoly players, and their competitions could extend for hours, with the unlucky figure—say, Frankie's Top Hat—going deeply into debt to Pearl's dainty Thimble or Iron. Their mother and father were downstairs in the kitchen.

The game had moved along quickly, with Frankie owning the whole line of properties between Free Parking and Go to Jail. He had hotels on all three reds—Kentucky, Indiana, and Illinois—as well as all three yellows—Atlantic, Ventnor, and Marvin Gardens. Pearl owned the pricey green properties, along with Park Place and Boardwalk. However, she had not erected any hotels or houses, to say nothing of the fact that her cash reserves had dwindled to fifty-five bucks, if Frankie didn't count the stack of singles.

"The next time you land on one of my hotels," he declared, "you're finished, kiddo."

"But you'll let me go into debt, won't you?"

"Hmmm. I'd have to think about that," Frankie announced. He prided himself on being a cutthroat Monopoly player.

"I could get lucky and miss your stupid hotels for a few rounds," Pearl said. "That might give enough time for my train to come in."

"Your ship," Frankie corrected her.

"What?"

"The phrase is 'for my ship to come in.'"

"I know," Pearl answered defensively. "That's what I said."

"No you didn't. You said, 'for my *train* to come in.'"

Pearl picked up the stack of Chance cards and began shuffling them unconsciously, which was a clear violation of the rules. "Slip of the tongue," she said.

Frankie smiled at his sister's nervousness. Looking down at the board with all his pretty hotels lined up, he figured there was exactly a zero chance of Pearl's ship coming in, or her train, or just about any other form of salvation.

Pearl replaced the stack of orange cards onto the game board. "I meant *ship*, of course," she said. "I meant to say *ship*."

If she hadn't repeated herself, it might not have dawned on Frankie that his sister was trying to pull a fast one, to cover something up.

Just then, they heard their parents' voices seeping out of the kitchen.

"If you're going to talk nonsense," Mr. Keenan was saying, "then this conversation is over."

Frankie and Pearl looked at each other, listening intently.

"Any place you can take our daughter, you can take our

son along too," Mrs. Keenan said.

"That boy's not grown-up enough to come with me. And I can take Pearl anywhere I want to."

"Over my dead body," Mother said.

Frankie reached out and swept up all his hotels off the board in one motion. "Let's be done, Pearl," he said.

"Okay," she agreed. And they concentrated on putting the game pieces into their box.

The voices from the kitchen had stopped now, but the silence was just as tense.

"I *did* mean *train*," Pearl whispered.

"What?" Frankie was lost.

"I didn't mean to say *ship*. You were right. I meant to say *train*."

As he put the lid on the Monopoly box, Frankie heard the kitchen door slam.

"Some 'Silent Night,' huh?" Pearl said.

"The Little Lord Jesus would have peed his swaddling clothes if he got born into this household," Frankie said.

"That's not nice," Pearl reminded her little brother.

"Nope," he agreed.

Six

P EARL TOLD FRANKIE EVERYTHING about Walking Mary. After Christmas vacation, in the first week of 1958, she interviewed the manager of the train station, Mr. Spencer, and Mr. Stimpert, their high-school principal, who doubled as Framburg's unofficial historian. She asked them questions about Walking Mary, and they appeared happy enough to talk to her. They thought it was nice to see a high-school student taking an interest in town history, even if Walking Mary seemed like an unusual starting point, and Mr. Stimpert tried to steer her investigation toward the famous Lincoln–Douglass debate held in an open field where the Union Dairy now stood. The only problem, Pearl told Frankie, was that none of her informants knew any more about Walking Mary than she did.

Her interview with Chief of Police Boomer Franklin showed more promise. She pressed him hard on the question of where Walking Mary slept each night, after the California Zephyr pulled through town at a minute past midnight. Chief Franklin loved the phrase "need to know." It was police talk, he explained, for divulging information only to those who truly needed to know said information. Chief Franklin could not ascertain the precise need-to-know basis on which Miss Pearl Keenan would be entitled to receive information regarding the woman known as Walking Mary, although "Walking Mary" would have to be considered an alias, strictly speaking.

When Pearl pushed the chief to answer whether or not any of his deputies had observed Walking Mary late at night, while cruising their squad cars in the vicinity of the train station, he told her, "Mind your own beeswax," and also "Don't poke your nose where it doesn't belong," which was a sure signal to Pearl that she was hot on the trail of what she *needed to know.*

Not everyone considered Pearl's investigation of Walking Mary a particularly good thing. Take her friends at Framburg High. As word got round that Pearl Keenan was hanging out with the town's crazy lady, you can't imagine what lowdown got whispered between hallway gossips and telephone breezers. At first, Pearl's friends just thought her kooky, which wasn't an altogether bad thing. Then, because she resisted any teasing and made the mistake of speaking up on behalf of Walking Mary, those same friends pronounced that Pearl Keenan's sentence was going to have to last longer and be harsher, continuing till dooms-day if that's what it took. Which made no difference to Pearl Keenan—who, by this time, considered her friends, even Francine, ignorant on the subject of Walking Mary, and she did not hesitate to share this conclusion directly with them.

Frankie did not like to hear his sister get insulted. Whenever he overheard a hallway reference to Walking Mary, Frankie felt the urge to grab a baseball bat, or maybe a hatchet, and defend his sister's honor with blood. Mind you, Frankie had never done this yet—defended his sister's honor with blood—but once the business with Walking Mary was out in the open, he came face-to-face with one fact about himself, both ugly and brave: Without knowing why, he had felt the urge to defend his sister's honor for as long as he could remember.

It made Frankie's blood boil to hear his sister's honor challenged. You'd think her stupid friends were casting his Pearl before swine, a phrase he'd lifted out of the Baptist Fellowship Bible.

Toward the end of January, Pearl came up with the

cockamamie idea of accompanying Walking Mary to inspect the California Zephyr at midnight and then following her home, wherever her home might be. Frankie happened to love cockamamie ideas, so when Pearl told it to him, in absolute privacy, he was one hundred percent in favor of this one. He wanted to go along himself, which Pearl overruled. Instead, Frankie agreed to serve as Pearl's lookout, which meant staying at home and handling the parents, in case they should need any handling, unlikely as long as they were asleep.

Pearl chose a Friday night, and it was snowing when she left the house at ten minutes past eleven, with Frankie sitting in the kitchen listening to WQFR radio.

Outside, to Pearl's surprise, it was not pitch black. Street lamps shone every half block. Snow was falling thickly. Frankie stood at the kitchen sink, looking out the window toward a street lamp, spotting snowflakes swarming like a monster cloud of summer gnats, only in wintertime. He thought momentarily of chasing after Pearl, but knew he wouldn't do it. She was determined to have this adventure alone, and he had his assignment.

As Pearl pressed forward down Burchard, right onto Lincoln past the old city cemetery, she debated the pros and cons of whether to show herself to Walking Mary at the train station or to follow her incognito after the departure of the California Zephyr.

Walking along Lincoln Boulevard, Pearl noticed that a surprising number of houses had their lights on, including front porch lights. Probably these people were nervous about accumulating snow and wanted to check the deepening amounts throughout the night.

Pearl felt her pace slowing down as she walked. Even in the twenty minutes or so she'd been at it, the snow had gotten deeper. Her legs were beginning to tire. It's tough to lift each leg a full foot out of wet snow, thrust it forward, and then plunge it down again into thick coldness. Snow clings to boots, makes them heavy. Some had wedged its way between the bottom of Pearl's slacks and the top of her boots, melting down her socks. Even though her legs were doing most of the work, and her hands and face were the coldest parts of her, Pearl's chest and arms began to ache, too.

Some of this she would remember to tell Frankie outright. Other details he could imagine on his own.

When Pearl came to the end of the cemetery she was halfway there, and it was just as easy to go forward as it would have been to turn around and go home. Which just goes to show how poorly Pearl was thinking at the time, because her calculation didn't include the necessity of walking all the way back home.

When she got to the downtown shopping district, Pearl stopped at Jim & Dot's Shell to check the time. The station was closed but kept its lights on, and there was an overhang above the gas pumps where she could get out of the driving snow. She pulled a mitten off and carefully wiped a finger across the face of her watch. Only ten minutes left until midnight, which meant she was definitely slowing down, so she tugged on her mitten and shoved off again.

Pearl had never seen downtown Framburg so abandoned. There were security lights on in some of the storefronts, but no one was around, absolutely no one. A single set of faint tire tracks in the snow circled the block of the courthouse, the first evidence of any traffic she'd seen. Probably a police car heading back to the station on Stephenson.

Pushing past the Sizzle Shop, she should have been within sight of the railroad tracks by then, but visibility was next to zero because of the falling snow. She knew she didn't have much farther to go. This was a good thing, because her chest was heaving from the effort of pulling each leg out of the snow and plunging it down in again. Pearl's face was dripping wet, partly from the flakes that washed continuously over her exposed skin and partly from perspiration. Her legs felt disconnected from her upper body.

Luckily, the depot was lit in every window, and there were a good half dozen street lamps illuminating the train platform. When Pearl got to the Buff & Puff, she could see the station looming through the snow squalls like a lighthouse beaming across rough seas. It must have been close to midnight, time for the California Zephyr to sound its whistle and activate the warning bells and gates. She worried that the train would come before she could make it to the other side of the tracks. There was no way she could run in these conditions, so she pressed forward, trying to make her legs move faster. Instead, they bogged down, moving slower and slower. Each step felt as if something were gripping the bottom of her boot from under the snow, pulling her down, not letting go. Foolishly, she shouted "Help!" into the wind. Who was supposed to hear her?

She was almost across the tracks, so near her destination, but the station kept receding from her vision. She could measure the vital signs of her situation by degrees of temperature, direction of wind, volume of snow, heart rate, and muscle ache. Pearl felt like she was slipping into dreamland, crossing the threshold into nightmare unreality. A sound came out of nowhere to startle her. A gong? A bell? A chime? It was midnight.

Pearl could not describe to Frankie what happened next. Everything following the stroke of midnight, when she crossed the railroad tracks in utter exhaustion, had to be pieced together from speculation. She must have made it across the tracks, because she had a vague memory of entering the train station. Her earlier indecision about whether to announce her presence to Walking Mary no longer mattered.

Pearl didn't recall actually going into the building, but obviously she must have, because she did remember seeing Walking Mary sitting on one of the polished wooden benches inside, the train clearly late. She was the only person there, and Pearl could tell the old lady was shocked to see her. *Shocked* probably isn't the right word, because Pearl had never seen this expression on Mary's face before or since. It was a portrait of genuine surprise, combined with bewilderment, and something else, too. Pearl concluded Walking Mary was actually frightened. Maybe she was scared of what it meant that Pearl should come out on a night like this to be with her.

What happened then requires two different explanations. Frankie says Walking Mary must have cast a spell over Pearl. Pearl's own explanation, less magical and more medical, was that she passed out from exhaustion and overexcitement. In either case, she had no recollection at all of anything that took place from that moment of seeing Walking Mary's face until she woke up at 6:00 A.M.

A CONVERSATION PEARL had a few days later with the night manager at the station confirmed that the California Zephyr did not arrive in Framburg until just past two o'clock that night, a couple hours late due to the weather conditions. He said that no Framburg passenger got on the train, and none got off. The Zephyr stopped momentarily, as its schedule required, and chugged off into the falling snow. "A total waste of my time," the manager complained.

He said he saw Pearl asleep on a bench in the station before the train arrived, and he figured she was waiting to board it. However, he claimed after the train pulled in and he returned from stepping outside to shout a hurried exchange with the engineer, Pearl was nowhere to be found. Disappeared.

To this day, neither Pearl nor Frankie can explain for sure how she came to wake up in the storage shed of the Sturgess Battery Company. Walking Mary was nowhere near strong enough herself to have carried Pearl there, even on a clear day. In a blizzard, through more than a foot of fresh snow, Chief Boomer Franklin could not have lugged an unconscious body from the station all the way beside the Pecatonica River up to the Sturgess Plant, equivalent of at least two city blocks. Nevertheless, Pearl got there, and that's where she woke up, inside the storage shed.

She was lying on an old cot with two thin army blankets spread over her. Somehow, her boots, hat, mittens, and coat had been removed. The cot was set in a dark corner of a cluttered room with a concrete floor and plain brick walls. A single bare lightbulb inside a wire-mesh cage hung from the ceiling in the center of the room. From its light, Pearl could inspect a jumble of old machinery, including two push lawn mowers and a small red tractor with a snow blade attached to the front, along with an assortment of rakes, brooms, shovels, spades, and a workbench covered with hand tools. The room smelled of grease and oil.

Aching all over, Pearl sat up and rested her stockinged feet on the cold floor. She stepped over to a metal locker and peered inside. There, hung on a hook, was her coat with her hat and mittens folded neatly across the top. Her boots were standing on the floor next to the locker in a puddle of water. Stuck to the door of the locker was a yellowed and frayed piece of paper. The printing on it was so old, it was barely legible. Columns of numbers signified times, and on top of one she could make out the word ARRIVALS. This very old train schedule was Pearl's first hint of Walking Mary's presence. She felt for her watch, took a couple of steps closer to the lightbulb, and read the time: five minutes after six!

Pearl heard a whistle from outside the building, so the train tracks had to be nearby. If it was 6:05, Walking Mary would already be at the station, ready to meet the Quad City Limited, first passenger service of the day connecting Chicago and Milwaukee with the Mississippi River towns of Moline, East Moline, Rock Island, and Davenport, Iowa.

Forget about tired legs. Forget about how cold her boots felt as she jammed them on, and how wet her coat still was. For the moment, forget even about Walking Mary and the train pulling into town. Pearl ran out of the building, got her bearings, and headed for home, running all the way.

Bursting through the kitchen door, Pearl saw Frankie standing at the sink. From his eyes, she could tell he'd been watching at the window for hours.

"No time to talk," Frankie snapped. "Get up into your room, and close the door till Daddy leaves."

Pearl slid out of her bulky coat and boots. "Who shoveled the driveway?" she asked.

"You did," Frankie lied. "Now scoot. We'll talk later."

AFTER BREAKFAST, Pearl took a long, hot bath, lying in the water with her head back, letting its heat seep into her muscles, letting its buoyancy hold up her spirit. She had to admit there was a lot she didn't know. On the other hand, she knew more than she could explain. She couldn't say, for instance, why she'd passed out in the train station at the stroke of midnight, or why she couldn't remember anything from that moment until she awoke in the Sturgess storage building. She couldn't say how she got there, but she had a pretty good idea. Walking Mary was the only explanation. It wasn't clear how a frail old lady could have carried the dead weight of a healthy teenage girl through thick snow over such a distance in the dark. But Pearl guessed that's exactly what had happened.

After her bath, Pearl sat down with Frankie, telling him everything exactly as she recalled it. And Frankie shared his concerns, including that more dangers lay ahead. "Even if Walking Mary isn't out to get you, Pearl," he warned, "that's not to say that somebody else isn't. I just have a bad feeling about this whole thing. People don't like you hanging around with Walking Mary. It makes them nervous."

Pearl listened to Frankie but did not respond.

"Oh," he remembered, "and Father asked where you were this morning. He said he'd checked your room, and you weren't in there."

Pearl sat up quick and stiff. "What did you say?"

"I told him you got up early to shovel the driveway."

"And he believed you?"

"Sure. Why wouldn't he believe me?"

Seven

To KILL TIME, FRANKIE and Pearl used to play a game they called Who Would You Be If You Could Be Anybody You Wanted to Be? In 1958, Pearl's favorite answers included Judy Holliday (Broadway star of *Bells Are Ringing*), Julie Andrews (in the television musical *Cinderella*), Ingrid Bergman (winner of the Academy Award for best actress in *Anastasia*), and whoever wrote the new book called *The Three Faces of Eve*, all about a woman with three personalities. Frankie favored Yul Brynner, Yogi Berra, and Major John Glenn, Jr., who set a speed record by flying from California to New York in a jet airplane in 3 hours, 23 minutes, and 8.4 seconds.

When playing the game, Pearl liked to imagine every aspect of a person's life—how she walked, how she talked, who her friends were, what kind of food she ate, whether she found spike heels comfortable, you name it. That was the whole point: to get inside the other person's skin, to live in their world.

After her all-night adventure, Pearl took a dramatic new step in following Walking Mary. Now she enacted the rules of their imaginary game in real life by outfitting herself closer to the way Walking Mary dressed. When meeting the Land O' Corn after school every day, Pearl wore a dress rather than her usual skirt and blouse or sweater. She wore her Sunday coat instead of a parka. Pearl hoped Walking Mary would take this gesture for what it was, a sign of love and respect, and not of mockery.

When Pearl climbed onto the station platform in her new getup, Walking Mary was already standing out in the freezing wind, waiting for the first signal of the train's arrival. As soon as Pearl noticed the old lady's bare hands, she removed her own mittens, stuffing them into her coat pockets. As Walking Mary spotted Pearl coming toward her, her wrinkled face smoothed into a wide smile. When Pearl stopped beside her, Walking Mary grabbed the girl's hand inside hers—an act accomplished with such ease and confidence, you'd have thought they were in the habit of holding hands every day.

Pearl tried a bold experiment. "Mary?" she said, trying to sound natural. "Remember Friday night?"

Walking Mary gave no indication that she understood or even heard Pearl's question. Still, she did not let go of the girl's hand.

"It was kind of a stupid thing for me to do, I know, to walk through a blizzard so late at night."

No response.

"I got so tired walking here through the thick snow that I must have fainted or something when I reached the station."

No response.

"When I woke up," Pearl said, "I was lying on an army cot in the storage shed of Sturgess Battery."

The moment Pearl specified the place, Walking Mary gripped her hand harder, as if stimulated by an electric shock.

"Well, I can't say for certain where I was," Pearl continued. "And it doesn't really matter. I sure wouldn't tell anybody."

Walking Mary relaxed her grip on Pearl's hand.

"Somebody took care of me that night. Somebody carried me there, laid me down, covered me up, kept me warm. Maybe that somebody saved my life."

No response.

"Thank you," Pearl whispered.

As soon as Pearl felt the first vibrations through her toes and feet of the incoming train, Walking Mary dropped her hand and reached up toward her face in the motion Pearl now recognized as fixing stray hairs. Automatically, as in a mirror, Pearl copied the same gesture. Then Walking Mary switched the umbrella into her left hand and reached back with her right to tap her leg. Quickly, Pearl did the same thing. Now Pearl realized the meaning of this gesture, too. Walking Mary was feeling for the seam down the back of her old-fashioned hosiery, making sure it was straight.

The train blew a loud whistle, and the door of the depot opened. Three or four people came out onto the platform, followed by the station manager.

"Maybe he'll come home today, Mary," Pearl whispered. "Maybe he'll be on the Land O' Corn."

Once Pearl saw that Walking Mary accepted her wardrobe of fancier clothes, it was easy to go all the way. In addition to wearing a dress, Pearl bought two pairs of nylons, took a black pen, and carefully drew a thin line down the back of each stocking so that her legs would match Walking Mary's. The girl continued to mimic the old lady's gestures before each train's arrival.

Eventually, Pearl went to the Goodwill store on Homer Street. The hat was no problem. For $2.75, she got a small blue one that fit snugly on her head and was not showy or likely to draw attention to itself. It was the kind that originally would have included a decorative veil over the front, which the wearer could pull back or down depending on the occasion. This was missing on Pearl's version, so she replaced it herself with a matching piece of netting purchased at Spencers for $.57. All told, her hat cost only $3.32, and Frankie didn't think it looked half bad. Pearl kept it in a box on the top shelf of her school locker, taking it out when she changed clothes in the girls' bathroom every day before walking to the station. She carried her school clothes to the station in a large shopping bag with handles. Just before returning home at the end of her daily routine, she'd stop either at Jim & Dot's Shell or at the Framburg Public Library to change clothes back again.

The coat was a bigger problem. Goodwill didn't usually carry mink coats, so she settled for an old wool one, brown, with a tattered fur collar. Four bucks. Then, as a finishing touch, she bought herself an umbrella.

Frankie could see his sister was becoming wrapped up, literally, in trying to become like Walking Mary. Pearl dressed like her, walked like her, gestured like her, and followed her routines. It was a real version of Who Would You Be If You Could Be Anybody You Wanted to Be? No different from what four-year-olds do every day when they try on Mommy's shoes or Daddy's hat.

Thinking back, Frankie couldn't believe his and Pearl's foolishness, their inability to see trouble rounding the bend. During the late winter of 1958, Pearl was having too good a time with Walking Mary to notice much else. It was as if Walking Mary had swung the door wide open into her life and was letting Pearl walk right in.

February was especially cold that year. Temperatures during the night would dip as low as two or three degrees. Sometimes, the mercury even fell below zero. If the wind was blowing hard out of the north, the outside air felt positively arctic. Over WQFR, Mr. Red Roscum kept warning Framburgers to take precautions against frostbite and hypothermia. Even Walking Mary adjusted her schedule to accommodate the cold.

Pearl had never known Walking Mary to approach the storage building at the Sturgess plant until after dark, when the employees' parking lot had emptied out. On frigid days, however, she headed to its shelter soon after the Land O' Corn pulled through. The first time Pearl followed her there went like a game of cat and mouse, because Walking Mary saw the girl tailing her and tried to lose her. She'd keep turning around to see if Pearl was still following a couple blocks behind. Pearl would just smile at her each time. Then Walking Mary would try picking up speed, to no avail. Eventually, she circled around the backside of Sturgess along the river and made a beeline for the storage building. Pearl narrowed the gap separating them and walked in a minute behind her, without knocking. To her surprise, Walking Mary didn't seem to mind.

In fact, Pearl concluded, it was a relief for Walking Mary to acknowledge where she lived. After that first time, she made no further pretense of ditching Pearl. If it was an extra-cold day, they'd just head over there together when the train departed. It would be dark because the sun sets so early in a Midwestern winter. Still, Pearl was able to sit an hour or more with Walking Mary before needing to head home herself.

They used two wooden packing crates as chairs and a wooden spool as a tiny table set between them. Eventually, Pearl saw what few supplies Walking Mary relied on for survival. She kept her possessions squirreled away in different hiding places around the storage room. There was a single-burner hot plate and an old tin pot for boiling water. These she kept in a cardboard box slid under the workbench on the cement floor. The other contents of the box included a tin of Lipton tea bags with a rusted lid, two china cups, both with chips out of their lips and one missing its handle, a china plate that matched the cups, and three forks. Why she had three forks but no spoons or knives, Pearl couldn't tell.

Pearl sometimes brought food, and Walking Mary kept this on a shelf of the metal locker. The old lady could make a single box of Ritz crackers last a month. Pearl guessed she kept them in the locker as protection from mice and rats, both of which she had seen scurrying along the floor of the building.

Pearl asked her once who else knew she lived there, but Walking Mary made no attempt to answer. Pearl and Frankie figured somebody else had to know. Even though Walking Mary occupied a very little space and wouldn't have disrupted the operations of a maintenance worker, there was no way she could have lived there for any length of time, much less for years, without somebody knowing it. Pearl promised herself to find out who was in charge of the building, but never got around to it. For the time being, she was happy to keep the secret to herself, and Frankie, of course.

Walking Mary and Pearl didn't go to the storage shed every day—only when it was extra cold. Maybe five or six times in all. Walking Mary boiled water for the two of them, and they shared a tea bag. The old lady offered Pearl Ritz crackers, but the girl only ever took one, not wanting to diminish the supply. Gradually, Walking Mary showed her other things, too. Like a can of black shoe polish and a rag, which she kept tightly wadded and jammed into a gap between two bricks. Like a yellowed bar of soap and another rag, lodged between the crosspieces of the army cot, presumably used for washing, although Pearl never saw her doing it. Like a little wooden top, the kind with a stick that you can spin between your fingers. It still had a few flecks of red and yellow paint on it, but mostly it was worn down to the bare wood. Walking Mary couldn't spin it herself on account of the arthritis in her fingers, but she beamed brightly when Pearl kept trying it till she caught the knack.

Then one day Walking Mary showed the girl what Pearl believed was her most prized possession. They were sitting on the two packing crates sipping very hot tea. Walking Mary had made it for them out of a bag that was already parched and puckered from an earlier use. While they sat there warming their hands on the cups before bringing them to their lips, Pearl was talking about Frankie, a subject Walking Mary always listened to with particular attention.

As Pearl chattered on, Walking Mary placed her cup of

tea on the wooden spool and reached her left hand over to the army cot, resting it on top of the blankets. Pearl hardly noticed the movement except to wonder why Mary wasn't drinking her tea. She kept burrowing with her fingers until she had worked them down beneath the blanket to the green canvas cover of the cot. All the while, Walking Mary kept nodding her head, listening to Pearl.

She leaned toward the cot and slid her hand deeper under the blanket. Then, like a magician in slow motion, she pulled a faded triangle out from its invisible hiding place.

"A flag!" Pearl said, announcing the obvious. "I didn't know you kept a flag under there."

Pearl reached her hand out to touch the red, white, and blue fabric, but Walking Mary pulled it away protectively. Then, thinking again, she extended the flag toward Pearl in both hands. She wanted the girl not only to touch it but to take it. She handed it to Pearl as if it were a sacred object.

Pearl took the tightly folded, triangular bundle from Walking Mary's hands and held it in her own. She didn't open it out. The flag had a surprising weight to it, and she caught from Walking Mary an attitude of reverence for the object. The fabric looked old, almost tired. Some of the stitching between the stripes had pulled loose. Pearl spotted a brown stain on a white patch.

"You've had this for a long time, haven't you?" Pearl said.

Walking Mary reached out again, and Pearl handed the flag back to her. She held it for a couple minutes before laying it on top of the cot. Pearl could only speculate where Walking Mary had gotten it or how long she'd had it with her. She treated it differently from any of her other possessions, indicating that it was the most valuable of them all.

When Pearl told Frankie this story, he was the one who pieced together what it meant. A triangularly folded flag is presented to the widow or mother of any soldier killed in war. Frankie said, "If it's as old as you say it is, I'll bet the flag comes from World War One."

"But . . ." Pearl objected, his point beginning to sink in.

"That's right," Frankie said. "Her son was killed, and she knows it."

"That makes no sense at all. Why would she still be waiting for him to come home?"

Eight

THE BEST TIME WALKING Mary and Pearl ever spent together was ice skating. They took to the ice on the frozen Pecatonica River right after the first of March. Most years, the river would be thawed by then, or nearly thawed. Certainly it would be too late for safe skating. But the winter of 1958 was so cold and so long that the Pecatonica didn't flow for good until April Fools'. There hadn't been a day above freezing through all of February, so the ice remained good and thick. Pearl couldn't say what put it into her head to take two pairs of skates to the train station that day. It was just a goofy impulse, she told Frankie later. In the morning before leaving for school, she took along her own skates from home and borrowed their mother's without asking.

She carried both pairs of skates in a brown grocery sack with string handles. Stuffed between them were four pairs of gym socks and two stocking caps. When Pearl showed up to join Walking Mary for the Land O' Corn, she didn't know for sure whether she'd suggest skating or not. Maybe it wouldn't be the right day, and she'd just carry the skates home again without opening the sack.

The train arrived on time, and they inspected it just like normal. By March, Pearl couldn't count how many days she'd checked the train windows with Walking Mary. When she first started making the rounds with her, Pearl looked at the old lady more than into the windows. Now, however, she mimicked Mary's concern and peered into each window individually. Pearl wasn't crazy. She didn't expect to see a soldier in a World War I uniform. But she had come to expect something special, to see something magical that would justify their daily commitment.

But there was nothing special on that train, just like every other day. As soon as any train pulled out, Pearl was in the habit of giving Walking Mary some extra space. She'd back away from her a few strides and let her deal by herself with the fresh grief of another day's loss. If the old lady's soul had a barometer, it must have swung crazily between high and low pressures, good and bad weather. It seemed Mary honestly brought fresh hope to each and every train, expecting this would be the one, and her beloved son would step off into her arms. And so, when he didn't, she must have experienced a change of interior weather so dramatic that it couldn't be charted on any spiritual map. She went from hope to despair three times a day. And then, three times a day, back again from despair to hope. Amazing.

When Pearl could tell Mary was ready to move on, she sometimes suggested they sit on a bench for a while and then go back to the shed for a cup of tea. Even in the coldest weather, they didn't risk that move until after all the Sturgess employees had gone home.

On this particular day, Walking Mary answered by heading for an outside bench around the corner of the depot, out of the wind. Sitting there together in silence, they could watch the frozen river.

"Did you ever go skating?" Pearl asked casually.

Walking Mary smiled, which the girl took as an affirmative answer.

"Did you enjoy it?"

She kept smiling. It must have been ages ago that she would have skated. By Pearl's calculations, Walking Mary had to be around eighty years old. Nobody knew her age for sure, and no amount of research had turned up anything definitive for Pearl. Still, if Mary's son was eighteen years old when he went into the army, and if that was in 1916, then he would have been twenty by 1918, when that war ended. And if Mary was about twenty years old herself when she gave birth to him, that would have made her forty in 1918. It was now 1958, forty years later, which would put her at eighty. Allowing for some reasonable adjustments to the figures, Pearl thought Walking Mary could be as young as seventy-five or as old as eighty-five. She couldn't have tied on a pair of skates for at least forty years.

"Me too," Pearl said. "I love to skate. It's one of my favorite things to do in winter. Better than sledding."

After an hour, they stood up together and walked slowly to the Sturgess plant, slipping through the door of the storage building. Mary poured water from the utility sink into her one tin pot, then boiled it on her hot plate for tea, breaking out a new bag for the occasion. Pearl didn't think of anything else to say that day, but neither of them minded sitting in silence. It was good just to be together.

The time ticked on.

5:30.

6:30.

Most days, when Pearl joined Walking Mary here, 6:30 was the latest she would allow herself to stay. She knew her folks would begin to worry.

"Mary, there's not a telephone in here, is there?" Pearl asked.

A look of confusion spread across Walking Mary's face. Surely, she knew what a telephone was, didn't she?

"Mind if I look around?"

Pearl got up and began to make a purposeful tour of the cluttered room. Other than the morning when she woke up in here alone, Pearl hadn't taken the liberty of looking around much. The two of them always sat in the same corner, where Mary's cot was. On the rare occasion that she disclosed another of her hidden treasures, it was always Walking Mary who got up to fetch the thing, not Pearl.

Sure enough, on the other side of the workbench, there was a black wall phone with a couple of oily rags draped over it, half concealing it. "Here we go," Pearl shouted across the room. "Do you mind if I use it?"

Walking Mary appeared agitated, probably because Pearl was shouting in a space that was usually stone silent. Then again, Pearl might have made her nervous by asking to use the phone. Walking Mary was careful never to disturb anything that didn't belong to her.

"It's a local call," Pearl said. "They'll never know."

Pearl removed the oily rags and tried not to let the receiver touch her ear or face as she dialed her number.

Mother answered, and Pearl told her she'd be home late tonight. She said she was studying at the Framburg Public Library, and she'd be home by 9:30. Then Pearl hung up without giving her mother a chance to object.

"I can stay longer, if it's all right with you," Pearl said, replacing the rags on top of the telephone exactly as she had found them.

Walking Mary stood up, rewrapped the Ritz crackers, and replaced the peanut butter jar on the shelf of her locker. Then, in apparent response to Pearl's question, she turned the hot plate back on and boiled them a second cup of tea.

They talked and talked. More accurately, Pearl talked and talked. She listened, too. Sometimes, as on this night, she told Frankie she believed she could read Walking Mary's body language so well that it seemed like *they* were talking. Of course, only one of them used her voice and said any words.

About 8:00, Pearl stood up. "Let's go skating," she suggested, and began pulling equipment out of the her grocery bag.

At the sight of two pairs of ice skates, Walking Mary smiled broadly. She probably thought Pearl was joking, and it was a good joke too.

"Come on," Pearl said. "I'm serious."

Walking Mary's eyes grew bigger in disbelief.

"I've brought two pairs of socks for each of us and a knit cap."

Walking Mary inched backward on her makeshift stool.

"You don't have to wear the cap if you don't want to. I just thought it might keep our ears warm. Come on, Mary, let's go."

Walking Mary smiled and shook her head no, as Pearl took the old lady by the hand, tugging gently.

"It'll be fun," the girl coaxed. "Nobody's on the river at this hour. We'd have it all to ourselves."

Mary's body offered some resistance when Pearl tugged at her arm, but not so much that she couldn't pull the woman up.

"What can it hurt?" Pearl pleaded.

Walking Mary continued to shake her head no as they walked out of the storage shed together and headed down to an old, abandoned pier on the Sturgess property. Pearl didn't know whether the battery plant had ever shipped products on the Pecatonica River, but the pier was made of steel and was still sturdy. It had a rusted sign that read KEEP OFF hanging cockeyed from a single nail.

Sitting on the pier, Pearl took off her shoes and began to

pull on two pairs of socks. "Come on," she urged, handing the woman the other two pairs. "Don't be afraid."

Surprisingly, Walking Mary took them. Pearl had the feeling they were alike in that regard. Nobody said "Don't be afraid" to either one of them without provoking a defensive reaction.

Walking Mary held the socks in her hand until Pearl untied her old black shoes and gently removed one and then the other. She placed both pairs of shoes in the grocery bag and then worked to pull on Mary's socks. Pearl doubted that Mary had ever worn a pair of athletic socks before.

Pearl laced up her own skates and then pushed and shoved to put her mother's on Mary's small feet.

Truth to tell, this was a lame-brain idea, and if Pearl had really thought it through, she'd never have suggested it. Asking a frail eighty-year-old to get up on ice skates— something she probably hadn't done since girlhood—ran a very high risk of breaking her hip or arm, or even causing a heart attack.

"Tight enough?" Pearl asked, double-knotting the laces.

Walking Mary nodded her head yes.

"Not too tight, are they?"

She shook her head no.

"Good. Now, do you want a cap or not?"

Walking Mary reached up and protected her own hat with her hands, which Pearl took to mean no. Pearl pulled a knitted cap down over her own ears and placed her formal hat carefully on top of their shoes in the grocery sack.

Pearl edged over to the side of the pier and stepped carefully onto the ice. It had a few ripples in the surface but was otherwise smooth.

"Come on, Mary," Pearl said. "Take my hands."

There was caution in the old eyes, but Walking Mary didn't hesitate to move. Luckily, Pearl was a strong skater and rarely fell. She and Frankie had spent countless winter days and evenings gliding on the Pecatonica since each was three or four years old.

When Walking Mary's blades touched the ice, she let out a kind of squeak or squeal, barely audible.

"Just hold tight to my arm," Pearl told her. "I won't let you fall, don't worry."

Gradually, Mary let go of the pier and grabbed Pearl's left arm with both of her hands. She had a good grip. They were standing next to each other on the ice.

"Easy does it," Pearl said and inched forward into a mini-glide.

Walking Mary did the same.

"There you go," Pearl urged her. "Move one leg and then the other."

On several of the first small strides, Mary lost her balance and Pearl had to catch her under the arm. Once, she nearly fell, swinging her whole body in front of Pearl's in a crazy spin. But Pearl held her up under both arms and straightened her to a standing position. The woman hardly weighed a thing.

It didn't take long, though, before she was skating with more confidence, matching the girl stride for stride. Pearl began lengthening their glides, pushing off the sides of her blades harder and harder.

Pearl encouraged her. "That's good, Mary. You must have been a wonderful skater when you were young."

The old lady squeezed the girl's arm tighter in confirmation.

At the start, they stayed within sight of the Sturgess pier, skating back and forth in lazy circles. But, after a while, sensing that Mary was strong enough to keep going, Pearl guided them gently toward the wider expanse of the Pecatonica's banks.

They skated under the bridge connecting the east and west sides of town. They skated past the parking area on the backside of the train depot.

As they went on, they found a sympathetic rhythm and began to glide together smoothly. They never let go of each other, but Pearl could feel Mary's growing confidence as she loosened her grip on Pearl's supporting arm.

The night sky was bright with a full moon and a heaven jam-packed with stars. They were the only skaters on the river. Pearl wasn't very good at telling distances. She thought it must be a quarter mile downriver from the train station to the Twin Caves. Maybe a little farther than that. The caves cut into the steep shoreline on the west side of the river, two limestone enclosures that opened onto the water. Father had told Pearl that when he was a boy, kids used to dive off the ledges inside the Twin Caves. Now there was no swimming allowed. Instead, people explored them in summertime by canoes that could be rented in Veterans' Park.

"Look, Mary," Pearl said. "Over to the right. It's the Twin Caves."

They skated in that direction, closer to the shore, etching graceful ovals in front of the caves.

Farther downstream, Pearl pointed out St. Felicity on the left. Its athletic field bordered the river. Even though all the kids who attended St. Felicity were white, the ancient school building sat on the east side of the river. While not nearly as old as the Twin Caves themselves, St. Felicity had to have been there when Mary's son was a boy.

With a little pressure on Pearl's left arm, Walking Mary—now Skating Mary—guided them into a looping figure eight next to the property of St. Felicity. As they glided, their blades making a rhythmic scraping sound against the ice, Pearl imagined herself standing on the east bank of the Pecatonica watching them. If all the nuns at St. Felicity weren't already in bed, one of them might have witnessed a miraculous vision: two skaters gliding arm in arm under the moonlight, both wearing formal coats over Sunday dresses, and ankle socks over old-fashioned nylons.

Come to think of it, maybe Pearl had joined the Order of St. Mary the Walker—wearing her habit, adopting her rituals, contemplating her faith.

They skated on and on down the river. A couple of times Pearl circled them back in the direction from which they'd come, but Walking Mary applied pressure to her arm and headed them forward again. Pearl wasn't worried about the time so much as she was concerned Mary might be getting tired. Apparently not.

The end of the line for skating on the upper river came halfway through Veterans' Park. At that point, when the water was flowing, there was a beautiful falls about six feet high and extending across the Pecatonica from one bank to the other. In winter, with the river frozen, the falls created a different but equal beauty. Its irregular rock formation was covered with ice and looked like some petrified scene out of a primordial Ice Age.

There was a long stretch of river between St. Felicity and the park, with pine trees and sumac bordering both banks. The route of the Pecatonica wound like a sleepy serpent through forested terrain. There were houses on both sides, but none of them was up against the river. The State of Illinois owned the east bank; the Illinois Central Railroad owned the west.

On the way to Veterans' Park, they skated under two more bridges. Occasionally, Pearl would see the reflection of a car's headlights on some nearby street, but throughout their entire skating expedition, she never spotted another human being. This whole world of ice belonged exclusively to them, a crystal paradise before the fall.

It must have been near nine o'clock when the river led them into Veterans' Park. Pearl knew she'd have to turn them around momentarily, both because they wouldn't be able to go much farther before hitting the falls, and because she needed to get Walking Mary back to the station well before the California Zephyr pulled in. She knew, too, that she had overstayed her promised return home.

In the middle of the park, the river widened into the area everyone called the duck pond, where Pearl had first encountered Walking Mary many years before. Skating around it now, she felt a sudden thrill of delight flow through her whole body—toes to ankles to legs and all the way up to the tiptop of her scalp. Unbelievably, she was skating with Walking Mary. Who'd have thought it? Who else in the entire town of Framburg would ever dare to think such a thing for themselves? They glided on in perfect symmetry, stride for stride, the two becoming one.

Then the most amazing thing happened. Just past the duck pond, where the river bent in a *V* and flowed under the park's magnificent bridge, Walking Mary pushed herself away from Pearl, letting go of the girl's arm, and skated free.

Pearl dug the side of her blades into the ice and came to a halt, sending a spray of fine shavings across the smooth surface. As Pearl watched Mary skate on her own, staring in awe, she began gliding slowly backward, feeling the reverse motion soothing the sore muscles of her legs.

At first, Mary skated in a large circle, down as far as the bridge and back to where Pearl was. Then Mary narrowed her pattern into an ellipse, making perfect arcs between the two banks of the river.

But she wasn't yet finished with her performance.

After a half dozen repetitions of the oval, Mary cut it in two, transforming the outer edges into a figure eight. As she crisscrossed the center of the pattern, she lifted both of her arms slowly to the height of her shoulders, then brought them down again to her sides. She repeated the motion time and again, lifting her arms higher each time, and bringing them back down with increasing force. She was skating faster and faster, flapping her arms inside that old mink coat—up and down, up and down. The old lady was skating with such ease, such grace, such power, that Pearl would not have been surprised if the blades of her skates had lifted off the ice, and she had glided into the air, defying gravity, gracing space.

This didn't happen. But by God, she did make a beautiful sight skating her mystical figure and exercising her mink-covered wings!

While skating all the way back to the Sturgess plant— out of Veterans' Park, between the forested banks of the Pecatonica River, behind St. Felicity, in front of the Twin Caves, under the bridges, and beside the depot—the two of them held each other's hands, cross-armed like a pair of lovers, like sisters.

Mr. Keenan was waiting for Pearl and Walking Mary at the Sturgess storage building when they returned from skating. Standing on one side of him was Chief Boomer Franklin, a hand resting on his sidearm, just in case. Standing on Father's other side, unbelievably, was Pearl's oldest friend, Francine, smiling.

Nine

ACTING ON A TIP from Francine, Mr. Keenan had learned about Pearl's alliance with Walking Mary several days earlier. When he found out the extent of the damage—how the old Negro had clearly *brainwashed* his daughter and, it might even be said, *kidnapped* her—Father thought it best to bring Chief Franklin and Pastor Weens into the picture. He was deeply grateful to Francine for stepping forward with this intelligence, "for Pearl's own good," and he wished his own children, either one of them, could show half the maturity of such a fine Catholic girl. (He would find a way to repay her, he vowed.) Clearly, Mr. Keenan told his wife, they had failed in their parental duties to bring up Pearl and Franklin in the fear of the Lord, and this was an opinion that Pastor Weens shared when he was called in to pray over the situation. There was no alternative but to crack down on both Pearl and Frankie, ground them to the house, limit their associations to approved friends, and restrict their activities to church-sanctioned fellowships. Mr. Keenan couldn't help commenting to Pastor Weens, as well as to Chief Franklin, that it was *Mrs.* Keenan who spent most of her time with the children and whose responsibility it was to set the primary example, to which the chief nodded in agreement. Mr. Keenan said, "Obviously, it's time I reasserted myself into my children's spiritual education." And Pastor Weens offered an "Amen" to that.

As for Walking Mary, Chief Franklin asked whether Mr. Keenan wished to press charges against the old lady for reckless endangerment, kidnapping, or any other possible "felonious infraction." The chief had no doubt of producing a conviction, "given Walking Mary's status in the community versus the clear innocence of your daughter, and considering the seriousness of the crimes." He opined that even a minimum sentence would "amount to life, given her age," either in the State House of Corrections or the Dixon State Hospital for the Mentally Ill, whichever the law determined more suitable.

When Pearl learned this, she begged her father not to press charges. She promised to do anything, anything at all, if he'd just leave Walking Mary alone. And, being a kind-hearted man, a Baptist, a deacon, a pillar of the church, as well as a loving father—as he would have his daughter know—he yielded to Pearl's wishes on one condition. "You must never see that woman again. You must never talk to her. You must never go near her. You must never mention her name again. If you disobey me in this, Pearl, I'll haul that Negro into court so fast. . . ."

"I promise," Pearl said.

With parental, civic, and religious authorities stacked up against her, there was no question of Pearl disobeying.

All the way from the beginning of March until the end of May, Pearl kept that painful promise. She did not return again to the train station. She did not go back to the Sturgess Battery storage shed. She did not speak about Walking Mary to her parents, and certainly not to anybody at Framburg High. She also did not sleep—at least not very much. And she did not eat—even less than normal. Had it not been for an occasional whispered conversation with Frankie, Pearl might as well have been sentenced to solitary confinement. Solitary, that is, if you didn't count Father's late-night visits to his daughter's bedroom, as when she was a little girl, "just to make sure you're all right."

FRANKIE WAS IN A FESTIVE mood when Mr. and Mrs. Keenan announced their usual Memorial Day picnic in

Veterans' Park, 1958. Given the incredibly tense spring, he thought this ritual might be canceled. But, no, the Fawvers and Sampsons would be there, as always. As well as other families from the Framburg Baptist Fellowship—the Mertons, the Coombers, and the Widow Elsbeck. Frankie's good mood appeared even to infect his sister with cheerfulness when he suggested they take a walk to the duck pond as the two of them had done so many years before.

Pearl asked permission from Father, who gave them stern instructions to return in fifteen minutes. Then brother and sister could enjoy a rare unchaperoned stroll.

All through that Memorial Day afternoon and evening, Frankie got the impression Pearl was making a real effort to be happy. He felt excited to see some return of his old sister who had disappeared nearly completely under the stiff penalty of their father's punishment. He knew how much Pearl missed her times with Walking Mary, but he didn't dare bring up the forbidden name. Not only was such conversation strictly prohibited but, Frankie figured, it wouldn't do any good anyway. Their father had Pearl trapped. There was no way in the world she could reclaim Walking Mary's friendship under the scrutiny of a police chief, a church pastor, watchful parents, and snoopy school friends. That happy part of Pearl's life, sorry to say, was over.

So Frankie was glad to see Pearl making an effort on Memorial Day. Maybe she was turning some kind of corner. To tell the truth, he had been worried sick about his sister. She'd begun to look more like a skeleton than any living thing. And her voice, on the rare occasions when she used it, had receded to a ghostly echo chamber, difficult even to hear.

At the pond, they laughed to see ducklings playing Follow the Leader with their mother duck. And they both enjoyed watching the older ducks maneuver to grab chunks of bread thrown onto the water by a couple of young children standing on the bridge.

When the family returned home that evening, Frankie risked suggesting a game of Monopoly, and he was shocked when Pearl nodded her agreement. It had been so long since they'd played—not since Christmas Eve—that it took him a while even to find the box. He didn't mind that she only competed halfheartedly, sometimes forgetting whose turn it was, and often neglecting to charge him rent when he landed on one of her properties. It seemed like a positive step for her to be playing the game at all. He felt encouraged.

At bedtime, Pearl did an unusual thing. She gave her brother a hug while saying good night. It was just a little hug, no big thing in any other family. But the Keenans were not huggers.

"Good night yourself," Frankie replied, wanting to hug his sister back, but feeling too awkward to give it a try.

He promised himself he would find the right future evening to return Pearl's compliment. The hug felt okay, something unspoken but trustworthy between brother and sister.

Frankie fell asleep easily and quickly that night. So he was startled when he heard a little knock—just a *tap-tap-tap*—on his bedroom door.

"Come in," he said, yawning.

His bedroom door swung inward, and Pearl stood in her nightgown, illuminated only by moonlight. "Are you awake?"

Frankie pulled himself up in bed. She tiptoed in, closing the door behind her. Pearl sat on the edge of his bed.

"Frankie?" she whispered.

He glanced at the clock on his bedside table. 11:11.

"Frankie? I need to ask you something."

He must have been deeply asleep because Frankie felt groggy and had to force himself awake. "What?"

"Does Mother ever come in here after you've gone to bed?"

"Huh?"

"Does she ever come in to visit you after you've gone to bed?"

"I guess so," Frankie said. "If she needs to talk to me."

"That's not what I mean," Pearl persisted. "I mean does she ever come in to *visit* you?" And she emphasized *visit* like it was a word composed of mysterious meaning instead of grade-school simplicity.

"I don't understand."

"I see her come in here sometimes, Frankie," Pearl continued. "And I hear the two of you giggling in here."

"When?" he asked.

"At night sometimes."

"Why, Pearl?"

"Because Father comes to *visit* me sometimes," and there she used that word again, and the repetition served to bring Frankie fully awake.

"What do you mean?"

"I mean . . . " Pearl said. But then his sister couldn't finish the sentence because she'd run up against what she'd come into his bedroom to say, and it was simply too horrid to utter.

"I'm sorry, Pearl. I don't understand."

"Are you sure Mother never *touches* you?" she asked.

Frankie wasn't stupid, of course, and this thing that had been lurking in the back of his mind for so long now came leaping out like a tiger. "Is that what Daddy does to you, Pearl?"

She didn't answer right away. And when she finally did, Pearl sounded apologetic. "I'm sure Father doesn't mean anything, Frankie. I was just wondering. We can talk about it another time."

Frankie nodded his head, confused, groggy. He yawned.

"Sleep well, little brother."

"You too, Pearl."

She tiptoed back to her own bedroom, careful not to wake their parents downstairs.

But Frankie did not sleep well.

IT WAS 11:50—TEN MINUTES before midnight—and something in Frankie's brain alerted him to trouble. He jumped out of bed and ran across to Pearl's room. His sister's bed was empty. She'd never even pulled back the covers.

Frankie slipped into the nearest clothes he could grab and skipped down the steps two at a time. Out the kitchen door, picking up his baseball bat from off the porch, and into the garage. He snatched his bicycle by the handlebars and yanked it around toward the street. He mounted like a cowboy in hot pursuit of some horse thief, pedaling so fast he could feel his heart beating. Nothing else was on Frankie's mind except to get to the train station before midnight, when the California Zephyr would pull into town. He didn't even notice, over his shoulder, the light go on in his parents' bedroom.

Frankie's bike rocked rhythmically from side to side—right, left, right, left—as he pumped for all he was worth. He stretched his fingers along the grips so he could hold on to the Louisville Slugger balanced across the handlebars. As he rode, Frankie tried not to think what he might encounter at the train station. He tried not to speculate what Pearl could be up to. Especially, he tried to shove out of his mind that maybe, just maybe, his sister's good mood earlier in the day had all been an act, something to throw him off the track. And what was that conversation about in his bedroom less than an hour ago? Frankie scolded himself. Why hadn't he been more alert? More careful? He pumped his bike wildly down Lincoln Boulevard. There was no car traffic to worry about. There was only a train schedule to meet.

With River Drive coming into view, Frankie could hear a car horn honking from behind. He was riding plenty far enough to the right that an automobile could pass, so he kept pumping at full speed.

Honk, honk!

Oh, for goodness' sake. "Pull around me," Frankie shouted into the night air.

A car pulled up on Frankie's left side, driving dangerously close to his bike. "Move over," he hollered without taking his eyes off the train tracks ahead.

A voice yelled at him from inside the car, "Franklin!"

He turned to look, still pumping away.

Father was behind the wheel. Mother was riding shotgun, with her window rolled down.

Frankie's heart was beating at a speed and with a power he'd never felt before. He thought he might almost outpedal his parents to their mutual destination.

As he pumped the bicycle ahead, pushing harder than he knew was possible, a train whistle blew, and the warning bells began to clang.

Frankie refused to slow down at his parents' warning but pumped his bike straight across the railroad tracks. The warning gates descended. From behind, he could hear Father slam on the brakes, and he glanced around just long enough to see the car skid to a stop on the safe side of the gate. Mother and Father jumped out of the car and ran across the tracks ahead of the oncoming locomotive.

Frankie jumped off his moving bicycle, grasping the baseball bat, and let his bike roll to a crashing halt beside the depot. He ran onto the platform and spotted Walking Mary standing alone, looking in the direction of the train's arrival. He sprinted to her side, startling the old lady.

Tonight, Frankie was too frightened for his sister to be scared of Walking Mary. He just blurted out, "Mary, I'm Frankie Keenan, Pearl's brother. Do you know where my sister is? She can't be here, Mary. She just can't be, or you're both in trouble!"

The sound of the incoming California Zephyr overpowered human speech. Its steely strength pulsed through the wheels into the tracks, shaking the ground on which they stood.

When the train jerked to a halt, three conductors stepped out of their passenger coaches. With the engine chugging, hoses vibrating, and steam hissing, the locomotive was full of suppressed energy.

Walking Mary did not respond directly to Frankie's question but took a quick look to her left and then back to her right. He could not say whether she'd even understood him.

"Please," he pleaded, seeing Mr. and Mrs. Keenan running toward them on the platform.

"Hold it right there!" Frankie's father shouted. "Where's my daughter? I'm not going to ask you a second time!"

Frankie watched Walking Mary straighten her hair, feel the back of her stockings, pull herself erect, and look up into the coach windows facing the platform. Mr. Keenan took one more threatening step toward the old lady and then, without warning, she grabbed her umbrella with both hands and gave him such a wallop across his stomach that he doubled over and fell to the ground, screaming in pain.

Walking Mary stepped past his crumpled body and began her inspection tour, peering into every window, heading toward the caboose.

Mrs. Keenan knelt down next to her husband, but she kept her eyes on Walking Mary. Mr. Keenan was struggling to catch his breath. "Sucker punched me," he spluttered.

"There, there," said Mrs. Keenan, sounding like a cliché character out of one of her books.

Frankie stood by helplessly, as did the train conductors, who seemed reluctant to intervene in a situation involving Walking Mary.

Walking Mary stepped down onto the gravel rail bed and crossed the tracks behind the caboose, out of Frankie's sight. He knew she'd be starting her return inspection back toward the front of the train along the opposite side of the coaches.

Mr. Keenan managed to get to his knees and then, with difficulty, to his feet. "Give me that bat, Franklin," he ordered.

"No, sir," Frankie said, gripping it at the handle with both hands.

"Come on, son. This is no time to play around. Give it to me. I'm gonna teach that old lady a lesson she'll never forget."

Frankie assumed a batter's stance, waiting for his father's pitch to cross the strike zone.

"You little bastard, you're worse than she is."

"No call for foul language," a conductor called out, picking up his step stool and hoisting himself back into the coach.

Frankie took a step back on the platform, away from his father and mother, and glanced toward the front of the train. There, stepping up from the rail bed, was Walking Mary, disappointed once again on her futile mission. As much as he would have liked to go straight over to the old lady to offer comfort, as his sister might have done, Frankie needed to keep a close eye on his father. If Mr. Keenan should grab the baseball bat out of his hand, there'd be no end of trouble.

Frankie kept a tight grip on the Louisville Slugger. His father showed no eagerness to walk down the platform and confront Walking Mary again without a weapon of self-defense.

The engineer blew an all-clear whistle, and Frankie looked again toward Walking Mary. Unbelievably, standing right there beside the old lady, was his sister Pearl. He never knew how she got there, or where she'd been hiding till that moment.

"Pearl," Frankie shouted, and took off running down the platform toward the two of them.

"Pearl Harbor!" their father hollered, limping along behind Frankie.

"Franklin!" their mother screamed, bringing up the rear. It wasn't clear whether she was calling after her husband or her son.

As Frankie approached Walking Mary, he could see Pearl was decked out as an exact replica of her old friend. He'd never witnessed his sister in her full Walking Mary attire—black shoes, formal stockings, Sunday dress, wool coat with fur collar, pillbox hat with veil pulled down over her face, and umbrella at her side. The two of them could have been twins. Or mother and daughter dressed alike for a formal portrait.

"Pearl!" he shouted. Suddenly, he felt so happy.

Without warning, Pearl raised the veil from her face, leaned down, and kissed Walking Mary on the lips. Then, showing no hesitation, Frankie's sister took two steps forward and one long stride down onto the tracks, directly in front of the locomotive. The whistle blew again, and the train lurched forward.

Frankie screamed, "No!"

Mother screamed, "Pearl!"

"Goddamned witch!" Father screamed.

What happened next defies belief, but Frankie saw it with his own eyes. He was standing not four feet from the scene, so he could see everything perfectly. The horror of the moving picture was so vivid that its memory recurred to him in slow-motion replay for years afterward.

Pearl stood calmly on the tracks, facing the California Zephyr, ready to die. The engineer blew his whistle long and loud, shouting in silent horror, unable to stop the locomotive in time to save the girl's life. Walking Mary, old and frail as she was, dropped her umbrella, leaped forward, and appeared almost to float down from the platform onto the rail bed, her tattered mink coat billowing out behind her. With the locomotive moving forward,

Walking Mary picked Pearl up like a baby, held her for just a moment in her arms, and then turned toward the platform, launching Pearl in a mighty heave toward Frankie. It would have taken the strength of Samson to do that. Pearl landed softly, without so much as a bruise, at Frankie's feet. He dropped his baseball bat and knelt down at his sister's side. Together, they watched Walking Mary disappear under the wheels of the locomotive with no chance of saving herself.

TIME AND EVENTS became a blur for Frankie after that. The train stopped about two hundred feet down the tracks. Chief Franklin arrived, along with his deputy. An ambulance came, but there was no one injured who required emergency care.

Frankie couldn't say for sure what happened to Father and Mother. He recalls grabbing his Louisville Slugger one more time in his right hand and picking up Walking Mary's discarded umbrella in his left. These were sufficient to discourage any more discussion with his father that night.

The next day, and for days to come thereafter, the *Framburg File* couldn't get enough of the story. Reporters chased down every imaginable lead—talking to Francine, Pastor Weens, Chief Franklin, the station manager, the engineer, a conductor, passengers who were eyewitnesses, the high-school principal, a psychiatrist from the state hospital in Dixon, and even the governor of Illinois, who was "happy the little girl was safe" and saw "no reason why this unfortunate incident should disrupt the peaceful relations between coloreds and whites in a model town such as Framburg."

But what no newspaper reported was the scene Frankie and Pearl both saw, kneeling side by side on the platform, holding onto each other, shaking in each other's arms. As the train backed up slowly from the tragic scene, brother and sister spotted a solitary figure farther down the tracks, walking away from the depot. Clearly, to both their eyes, it was Walking Mary. At first, she was walking alone, slowly, deliberately, without turning back. Then, gradually, a second figure appeared out of the night mist and fell in step alongside her, a tall slender figure in military uniform. Walking Mary slipped her right hand into his left arm as they walked together, yet farther and farther away. Frankie, usually so good with vocabulary, could not conjure the proper words to describe the scene—not then and not later—although he and Pearl would share this secret vision for the rest of their lives. Eventually, Walking Mary and her son were joined by others. But by then, the portrait was too far removed even for Frankie's well-known imagination to describe with exactness. The best he could do was to cop a phrase from their Baptist Fellowship's Bible-in-the-Pew: Walking Mary became surrounded by "a cloud of witnesses." Between brother and sister, for their lifetimes to come, this would have to do.